The man did crazy-good things to her....

Macy had no desire for anything complicated. As long as they were discreet, no one in town would know. Friends with benefits. She'd never really had one of those.

"Why are you looking at me like that?"

She blinked and realized she had been staring at Blake. "Uh...you're very handsome."

That sly grin spread across his face. "Okay."

He turned back to the computer, but continued to grin. He knew.

"You do bad, bad things to me, Mr. Marine."

The grin grew bigger.

"I haven't touched you," he said, his eyes still staring at the screen.

"Oh, but you don't even have to," she whispered. Maybe she had had one too many glasses of wine with the dinner. The room was too warm....

That made him turn.

"Ms. Reynolds, are you coming on to me?"

"Yes, sir. I believe I am.... So what are you going to do about it?"

Dear Reader,

It's funny how love can find us at the oddest times. When I met my husband in college, I'd pretty much given up on men. He and I became best friends, and I believe, in part, that's because I wasn't really looking for love. It found me.

The last thing Blake Michaels, a marine returning to his small Texas town, needs in his life is a hardheaded woman with issues. That's exactly what he gets when he first meets publisher Macy Reynolds, who has a soft spot for giant Great Danes and wounded heroes.

When Macy and Blake butt heads, sparks fly. But the chemistry is undeniable, and what they don't realize is they are exactly what the other needs. Having these two fall in love was the most fun I've had in a long time. I hope you enjoy *Her Last Best Fling!*

And to all of our military personnel around the world, thank you for everything you do.

Candace Havens

Her Last Best Fling

—

Candace Havens

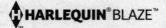

H HARLEQUIN® BLAZE™

PLEASE RECYCLE · THIS PRODUCT IS RECYCLABLE

Recycling programs
for this product may
not exist in your area.

ISBN-13: 978-0-373-79778-3

HER LAST BEST FLING

Copyright © 2013 by Candace Havens

HARLEQUIN®
www.Harlequin.com

Printed in U.S.A.

ABOUT THE AUTHOR

Award-winning author and columnist Candace "Candy" Havens lives in Texas with her mostly understanding husband, two children and three dogs, Harley, Elvis and Gizmo. Candy is a nationally syndicated entertainment columnist for FYI Television. She has interviewed just about everyone in Hollywood, from George Clooney and Orlando Bloom to Nicole Kidman and Kate Beckinsale. You can hear Candy weekly on The Big 96.3 in the Dallas-Fort Worth area. Her popular online writer's workshop has more than two thousand students and provides free classes to professional and aspiring writers. Visit her website at www.candacehavens.com.

Books by Candace Havens

HARLEQUIN BLAZE

To get the inside scoop on Harlequin Blaze and its talented writers, be sure to check out blazeauthors.com.

Other titles by this author available in ebook format. Don't miss any of our special offers. Write to us at the following address for information on our newest releases.

Harlequin Reader Service
U.S.: 3010 Walden Ave., P.O. Box 1325, Buffalo, NY 14269
Canadian: P.O. Box 609, Fort Erie, Ont. L2A 5X3

For those in the military and police and fire departments, who put their lives on the line for us every day.

1

AFTER NINE MONTHS of hell in the Middle East—stuck in a hot, dark cave—Blake Michaels welcomed the deluge pounding his windshield. Heavy rain might keep the curious townsfolk from showing up at the Lion's Club. His mom had moved the party when she discovered a good portion of Tranquil Waters wanted to be there for the hero's return.

He was no hero.

He was a man who served his country, and happened to be in the wrong place at the wrong time.

The gray, wet weather mirrored Blake's mood. He wasn't fond of crowds, at least since he'd returned to the States. The time away had changed him in ways he'd only begun to explore.

He appreciated the thought of a party in his honor, but being around that many people at one time was enough to give a guy the cold sweats. His doctors had promised the anxiety would eventually pass. Almost a year in solitude with only a guard, who never spoke for company, had left him with a few issues.

Once, in the hospital afterward, the nurses had found him huddled in a corner of his room. He never wanted to repeat that night.

He'd had a complete blackout, an "episode" they called it, and it scared the hell out of him. That was when he started to take the therapists more seriously.

As he came around a curve on the highway, a flash of white popped up before him. Brakes squealed as his Ford slid to a stop. His breath ragged from trying to steer away from the woman and the giant animal struggling against her. She held the animal while simultaneously trying to push its hindquarters with the toe of her candy-red high heels into the backseat of her car. This was a problem as her tight pencil skirt only allowed her leg to move to a certain height.

Crazy woman.

The dog outweighed her by at least fifty pounds. She'd have better luck putting a saddle on the black-and-white creature and riding to wherever she wanted it to go.

If they didn't get off the two-lane road fast, someone would plow into them. No way would Blake allow that to happen.

A dog isn't worth her losing her life.

He paused for a second.

Dang if he wouldn't have done the very same thing. He loved animals. Scotty, the therapy dog at the hospital, gave him hours of companionship while he went through the hell the docs called physical and mental therapy.

Straightening his truck on the shoulder, Blake hopped out.

"Here," Blake said as he shoved the beast into the back of the Ford SUV.

As he did, the woman teetered on her high heels and fell back. He caught her with one hand and pulled her out of the way. Slamming the door with his foot so the dog couldn't get out, he steadied her with his hip. Pain shot through his leg, and he sucked in a breath.

"Are you okay?" He kept her upright with his hands around her tiny waist. The sexy librarian look with the falling curls hiding her face, nearly see-through, rain-soaked blouse and tight skirt over sexy curves did dangerous things to his libido.

Down, boy. Down.

"Thanks," she said as she glanced back at the dog. "I'm fine. I better get Harley back to the shelter. This is the second time this week she's broken out. Her owner passed away, and she keeps trying to go home. If you ask me, it's the saddest thing ever to see an animal suffer." She waved her hand. "Well, there are worse things in the world, but it's sad that she doesn't understand that he's gone."

"You could have been killed," he said through gritted teeth, although more from the pain in his leg than being upset with her.

Stiffening, she turned slowly. When their eyes met, a clap of thunder boomed. She jumped and stumbled. He held on to her to keep her from falling down.

Tugging out of his grasp, she raised an eyebrow. "Yes, I'm aware of the danger." Her chin jutted out slightly. "Which is why I stopped to get the dog. She was a danger to anyone else who might cross her path. Thank you for your assistance."

He'd offended her without meaning to. The nurses were right, surly had become his natural state. "I—uh…" He wasn't sure if he should apologize. With his luck, he'd only make it worse.

"Mr. Clooney's rooster Pete says the thunderstorms are going to be pretty bad the next couple of days," she said as she climbed into the vehicle. "And that darn rooster is never wrong. Perhaps you should think about staying inside so you aren't tempted to help poor defenseless animals."

With that, she slammed the door shut.

Did he just get the brush-off?

Mr. Clooney's rooster? Wait, how was that annoying creature still alive?

He remembered when his brother poured half a bottle of cold medicine in the rooster's feed so they could sleep in one morning during the summer. If anything, the somewhat drunk rooster crowed even louder the next morning.

The SUV sped off toward town.

Yep, that was definitely the brush-off.

It'd been a while since he'd spent time with a woman. Well, besides, the doctors and nurses at the hospital. He'd done four tours in a row, only taking a few months off occasionally to see his mom while trying to forget everything he'd gone through the past two years.

This final tour was one he couldn't put on the "man shelf." That's what his therapist, a woman who was exceptionally bright and never let him get away with anything, had called his ability to shove things that upset him to the back of his brain. Every time he tried to redirect the conversation away from his recent past, she called him on it.

Blake shoved a hand over his newly shorn hair. He'd let it get longer in the hospital, but his mom didn't like it that way.

And hell if he wasn't just a big ole mama's boy. Blake and his brother, J.T., would do anything for her. She'd held their family together after their dad died when he and J.T. were teens.

He might not like the idea of the party, but eating home-cooked meals his mom made was high on his list of favorite things. He could suffer through any inconvenience for that.

Thunder hit again, and the black-haired woman's heart-shaped face popped into his mind with those almost-translucent green eyes that had seen too much of the world. He wondered if the thunder might be an ominous sign that he should stay away from her.

He grinned.

Nope, that wasn't going to happen. The last thing he needed was to chase some skirt, but there was something about her. She'd been dressed sexy, but she didn't suffer fools gladly.

That was something he admired.

He liked a challenge. This was a small town, and he was about to be at a party with some of the best gossips in Texas—and that was saying something in this state. A type like the sexy librarian would surely be a topic of conversation. His mom hadn't mentioned anyone moving into town during their chats, so the woman had to be fairly new to Tranquil Waters.

After parking the truck in front of the Lion's Club,

he ripped off the wet shirt. He had an extra hanging in the cab. Once he was dressed in his blues, he steeled himself for the oncoming tide of good wishes.

"For he's a jolly good..." voices rang out as he swung open the door and stepped inside. In other circumstances, he would have run back to the truck. But he smiled and shook hands, all the while thinking about that woman with the raven hair and killer red heels.

Perhaps having half the town at his party wasn't such a bad thing.

Facing the blue-haired gossip brigade, he gave them his most charming smile.

"Ladies, you haven't changed a bit," he said. "If I didn't know better I'd guess you were selling your souls to keep that peaches-and-cream skin of yours."

His mother rolled her eyes, but stood on tiptoes to give him a hug.

"You're up to something," she whispered.

Oh, he was definitely up to *something*.

"BRAN MUFFINS AND fake butter. That was one knight in shining armor," Macy complained to Harley as she wrapped wire around the lock on her cage. She never swore around the animals in the shelter as she believed they'd been through enough trauma, without listening to her temper tantrums. So when she wanted to use angry words, she thought about foods she hated.

"Doesn't it figure that ten minutes after I vow no more men forever, he shows up?"

The dog made a strange noise that sounded like

"yes." Great Danes did have their own language. And she bet Harley understood every syllable she said.

"Oh, no. He has to be so hot that steam came off of him. And me." She fanned her face. The heat from the encounter still on her cheeks.

"Here he comes galloping on his horse to the rescue." Macy's last two relationships were nonevents, except for the part where they'd cheated on her. Three weeks ago she'd discovered the man she thought she might marry was having what he called "a meaningless relationship" with an intern at the paper.

Well, it had meant something to Macy.

Harley made a strange sound.

"Fine, it was a truck he galloped in on, but still."

The dog whined again.

"Lovely girl, I'm sorry. I've been going on and on about me, when you have much more to be sad about." She squatted as much as her skirt would allow and petted Harley through the kennel.

The handsome face of the knight was one she recognized. Though his dark brown hair had been cropped close to his head, it was those dark brown, almost-black eyes she couldn't forget. The marine, who'd been captured in Afghanistan, had returned home. She'd been headed to the welcome-home party to cover it for the newspaper. That wasn't the kind of thing publishers did at larger papers, but this was a small town. Darla, the reporter assigned to the story, had to pick her kid up from school and take him to the dentist. And the other two reporters had the flu.

Thinking that it would be a quick in-and-out, Macy had decided to cover the party.

Well, until she found Harley soaked to the skin.

She loved animals. They weren't as judgmental as humans. Since she was sixteen, she'd been volunteering at various shelters around the world. Every time she took a new job, that was one of the first things she did. Well, except for when she was in the Middle East. She didn't have time to breathe then, let alone help anyone else.

In the newspaper business, one had to move a lot. There was constant downsizing and she had to go where the jobs were. That was how she'd landed in Boston—until the fiasco that was her almost-fiancé throwing their comfortable life into the proverbial toilet.

Harley nudged her.

"I promise as soon as the fence guy gets done, you are moving in with me. If this rain would stop, they could finish." This was the first pet she'd ever adopted. The old girl had one green and one blue eye. The sorrow in them tore at Macy's heart. She was an orphan, too, and she'd bonded with the dog ever since she'd caught her trying to get back home the first time.

Her great-uncle Todd, who had been Macy's only remaining relative, had willed her the town's newspaper. For months she'd been trying to sell it with no luck. When she walked in on her ex and his meaningless plaything, she decided moving to a small locale wasn't such a bad idea. Along with the paper, her uncle had left her a beautiful house overlooking White's Lake. She'd decided to put an eight-foot fence along two of the four-acres of the property so Harley would have a place to roam.

"Great Danes need a lot of space." She smiled and scratched the dog's ears.

"Hey, I thought you went to the party," said Josh from the door as he slipped booties over his shoes for sanitary purposes. He was the local veterinarian who donated his services to the shelter.

"I was on my way, but Miss Harley got out again. I caught up with her on the highway."

Josh tickled the dog under her chin, his fingers poking through the cage. It was a large eight-by-eight-foot space, but it wasn't big enough for the hundred-and-seventy-five-pound dog.

"Nice knot with the wiring there. Do you sail?" He pointed to the impenetrable knot she'd devised to keep Harley in.

She shrugged. "Something I picked up from my dad. In the summer we'd go sailing." Those weeks were some of the happiest of her life. Her parents were journalists, so it was in her blood, but it meant they traveled the far ends of the earth, leaving Macy at home.

"So are you heading over to the hero party?"

Feeling as if she'd stood in a rainstorm for an hour, which she did, she decided she'd be better off going home. "No, I'm heading back to my place to change."

She noticed Josh wasn't meeting her eyes. He did everything he could not to look at her.

She glanced down. Her white blouse was completely sheer and she was cold.

Great. Wonderful. Lovely.

"Well, Cecil is up at the front, so I guess I'll be going," she said as she made a quick exit.

Josh was a nice guy. They'd even tried to date once. But discovered there was absolutely no chemistry, which was probably why he was doing his best not to look at her nipples protruding through the sheer fabric of her shirt and nude-colored bra.

Unless she wanted to be the fodder for more town gossip, there would be no party in her future.

The lovely scent of wet dog pervaded her senses as she made the short drive home.

Five minutes later, she turned on the fireplace in the main family area. The front of the place had a Gothic Revival exterior. The back was full of windows. She loved the water. Living near it made her feel close to her dad.

After constantly chasing the next big story, the pace of Tranquil Waters nearly killed her at first. But she'd grown accustomed to the quiet. Her whole life she'd heard Texans were incredibly kind, and they were— However, the ones here didn't trust outsiders, especially Yankees, of which she was one, having spent most of her formative years in the Northeast.

A hot shower was in order. Then she'd bundle up and see what Mrs. Links, the housekeeper who worried that Macy was wasting away, left in the fridge for dinner. The housekeeper came in three times a week, even though Macy was perfectly capable of cleaning up after herself.

Mrs. Links was another part of her strange inheritance from Uncle Todd. He'd provided for her weekly allowance until the time she no longer needed employment.

Macy didn't have the heart to ask the nearly seventy-five-year-old woman when that might be. For someone who made a living by asking the tough questions, Macy had a soft spot when it came to animals and her elders.

As the warm water sluiced across Macy's body, her mind drifted to the marine. Those biceps under her hands were of a man who wasn't afraid of hard labor. Marines had to stay fit, and she had a feeling he'd have washboard abs, as well.

Men with great abs were her weakness.

You swore off men.

The smell of his fresh, masculine scent. Those hard muscles, the warm smile, even after all he'd been through.

The blood thrummed through her body.

She hadn't been with a man in what felt like forever. That was all. He was hot, and any other woman would feel the same way after looking into those sweet chocolate-brown eyes.

Turning down the water's temperature to cool her body, she wondered how long she'd be able to resist the marine.

2

VIOLENT THOUGHTS CROSSED Blake's mind as Mr. Clooney's rooster crowed, waking half the town—so much for the extra rest. Shoving the pillow over his head, he closed his eyes and willed himself back to the dream about the woman in the red heels. The rooster crowed again.

"I'll kill that bird some day," he growled as he rolled out of bed. Too many years in the military had him up, showered and sipping coffee ten minutes later.

His mother had taped a note to the fridge that said, "Muffins are in the warming drawer. Love, Mom."

At five in the morning, she'd probably already been at the feed store for at least an hour. She liked to get the paperwork done before the place opened. Even though she didn't need to be there anymore, she'd insisted on keeping the books and visiting with customers when they came in. She'd built the business from the ground up while his father traveled the world with the military. She believed in having roots and wasn't much for leaving the town she was born in. Their relationship worked, because when they were together, they treated each other as if no one else existed in the world. Well, except for Blake and his brother.

Their parents made certain their boys had an idyllic childhood in the town centered between two lakes. They lived on the edge of town, which had exactly four stoplights, a couple of grocery stores and various shops on the rectangle, as they liked to call it. When the town was first built, there was no real plan. When they finally decided they needed a courthouse it was built in the heart of the rectangle of shops and businesses.

But Tranquil Waters had changed while he was deployed. He remembered laughing about the letters from his mom talking about how the town council had decided that they could have a Dairy Queen and a McDonald's on the same side of the highway.

They also—thanks to the lakes and artists and writers who populated the town—had a good tourist industry year-round. It was almost Halloween and he hadn't seen a house yet that hadn't been decorated. There were several haunted B and B's and even a large corn maze on the Carins' pumpkin farm.

Everything seemed so simple in a small town. It didn't take a CIA spook to find out that the woman he'd run into on the highway was the new publisher of the town newspaper.

"That Yankee girl just doesn't understand our ways," complained Mrs. Lawton. "She reported that old Mr. Gunther was thrown in jail Saturday night.

Well, everyone knows he's spent every weekend in that jail cell for the last twenty years. Ever since his sweetheart of a wife, Pearl, passed—God rest her soul—he's just been longing for her. Poor man. What he needs is a new woman, a younger one to keep his mind off his troubles."

While she had glanced around at the other women in her circle, Blake had a feeling she wanted to be the new woman to occupy Mr. G's thoughts. Blake grinned as he sipped his punch. Didn't matter that she'd just turned eighty-five and Mr. G had to be nearing a hundred.

"She has that huge house, darn near a mansion," Lady Smith chimed in. Her name was Lady, and for some reason everyone in town called her Lady Smith. Out of respect, and the fact that she was a friend of his mother's, Blake had once called her Mrs. Smith when he was about ten. She'd scolded him and told him she was a Lady, and he'd do well to remember that in the future.

The town was full of oddballs, and he'd been one of them. As a kid, he'd run around dressed like Davy Crockett for two years and no one had said a word. Apart from his brother, who was more a Spider-Man fan.

"She's got more money than she knows what to do with. Imagine, putting the paper on the inter— whatever those kids use nowadays," Lady had complained. "People here like to hold a newspaper in their hands. And she doesn't seem to understand that there are some stories that just aren't fit to tell. I've written countless letters to the editor, but she never prints or listens to them." Lady waved her hand in the air dismissively.

"Darn Yankee."

How dare she tell the truth about Tranquil Waters. The nerve of the woman. Blake found himself chuckling as he rinsed his cup in the sink.

His mother probably didn't need his help at the feed store. But he didn't want to sit around stewing. It almost always sent him in the wrong direction.

He wondered where Macy—he'd finally learned her name—might be. Likely still in bed, if she were smart. Any sane person would be at this hour of the morning. Pulling the truck out of the drive, he saw something run past.

Blake blinked a few times and followed the blur. "It can't be."

The monster dog he'd recently stuffed into a car sat on the porch of a white-framed house with a for-sale sign in the yard. The spot was about five blocks from his mom's house.

The way Harley stared at the door, as if willing it to open, broke his heart. Blake had seen a lot of awful things through the years, but kids and animals in distress were his weaknesses. He'd do anything to protect them.

Macy was right. Unlike a human, the dog couldn't understand her master was gone.

Exiting the truck slowly, he stepped up the stone path. She glanced back at him, with the saddest puppy eyes. One of the eyes was blue, the other green.

He hadn't seen her eyes when he'd been dealing with the hindquarters.

"Hey, pretty girl, what's up?"

He held out his hand, but she turned away from him. Lifting a large paw, she hit the doorknob.

Damn dog. His heart lurched. Not sure what he should do, he sat down on the top step next to her. He could drag her to the truck, but he didn't have the nerve. If he gained her trust, maybe she'd go willingly. He had a feeling being at the house was about more than just returning to where she felt safe.

"I'll sit here with you until you decide what you want to do next," he said softly. He didn't have anything better to do.

The dog pawed at the door again and growled.

Blake leaned back against the railing. He could have sworn the dog said, "Let me in."

I am losing it. Now dogs are talking to me.

"Did you just say, let me in?"

The dog pawed his shoulder.

Yep, he was crazy.

"Oh, girl, sorry, I don't have a key. I'd let you in if I could, but I don't have one. And I have a code I live by. Breaking and entering isn't an option."

She barked and then leaped off the porch.

As quick as his sore leg allowed him, he got up and followed her around the side of the house.

When they reached the back porch, she pawed at the door handle and attempted to open it with her mouth. She snarled when it didn't budge.

"Well, we tried," he said.

She cocked her head, and he swore she rolled her eyes.

Taking off to a chipped birdbath in the middle of

the lawn, covered with dirt, she pawed the rocks surrounding the base of the concrete fixture and barked. Blake limped out to the fountain, more to appease her than anything.

There on the ground was a key.

"Okay, dog. Now you're freaking me out." If she had had two legs instead of four, she could pass for human. And she had to be one brilliant pup to relate the key to the door.

As he unlocked the door, he noticed someone peeking over the fence.

He pointed an accusatory finger at the dog. "Fine, but if we get arrested you're taking the rap." He patted her on the head. Before he could turn the knob and open the door himself, she nosed it open and stood in the small kitchen, as if waiting for him to come inside. Once he was in, she closed the door with her nose.

Blake had never seen such a thing. The few dogs he'd had when he was a boy could sit and lie down, but that was about it.

Harley woofed and trotted to the living room, where she sat in front of a wingback chair. She nodded at him, as if she wanted him to sit down in it. More out of curiosity than anything, he did. A paw shot out and pushed so hard on the chair he worried he'd go head over heels.

But he didn't fall.

The dog ducked beneath the chair and tossed out several stuffed animals, a ball and chew bones that had seen better days. Once she had her stash from under the chair, she moved the items one at a time to the charcoal-gray sofa. The booty soon became a pillow as she lay atop her toys, sighing as if she'd been on a long journey.

"Poor girl," Blake whispered. The sight of her relaxing choked him up.

"That's the first time I've seen her sleep since he passed," a feminine voice whispered.

Head snapping around, he took in Macy Reynolds's tight jeans, pink hoodie and those furry boots women wore when the thermometer dipped below seventy. The town was having an unusually cool October, and the temperature hung around the fifty-degree mark. A sleepy angel with no makeup, and more beautiful than she'd been the day before.

"I saw her running past my mom's house when I left this morning and I decided to follow." He held up a hand. "I swear she made me unlock the door. She showed me where the key was."

"I believe it. Evidently the drama was about her missing toys. I don't blame her," Macy continued to whisper. "I'm kind of fond of my stuff. I don't have that much, but what I do have is precious to me."

Odd since he'd learned she inherited her uncle's house. He assumed she had tons of stuff.

"What?" She checked her clothing as if she might have missed a button.

"Nothing. I…heard last night that you inherited your uncle's new mansion."

She scrunched her face. "Yes, he— Yes."

"For the record, I haven't been stalking you. Some of the gossips at the party were talking about it."

She smirked and moved to the sofa to sit beside Harley.

"Is there an expiration date or something on being the subject of town gossip? I've never lived in a place where other people were so in your business. Usually, as a reporter, I'm the nosy one. It's disconcerting. And I don't think they like me very much, although I'm doing my best to turn their local into a paper that resembles more than tractor reports."

He laughed, and the dog opened an eye and glared at him.

"Unfortunately, until the next interesting person moves to town, it'll be all about you."

"Yes, but the hero has returned." She nodded in his direction. "Can't you be the subject of conversation for a while?"

"Nah. I'm not nearly as interesting as a Yankee woman who wears pencil skirts and sky-high heels. And according to the gray hairs, you have a scandalous past where you combed the world reporting on everything from celebrities to wars. Some man broke your heart, and you're here hiding away."

Her eyes opened wide. "Wow. They are good. I wish they'd be as generous with their words with me. Honestly, I know heads of state who give more in an interview than people in this town."

She hadn't bothered to deny any of what he'd said, so it must have been true about combing the world and the man who was in her life. He wondered if that relationship was really over. He shrugged. "Give it some time, they'll come around."

"Will you talk to me?"

He frowned. "I thought that was what we were doing."

"No—I mean, yes." She waved her hand. "In an interview. The *Tranquil Waters News* should do a feature on the town hero."

That was the last thing he wanted.

"There isn't a lot these folks don't already know. I've been gone for about seven years. I'm back, a little worse for the wear but alive. There isn't much more to tell. I was doing my job but happened to be in the wrong place at the wrong time."

She sighed, not unlike the suffering sound the dog had made. "I should have known. You're no different than the rest."

The disappointment in her voice forced him to do something he promised he never would.

"All right, if you want to talk, that's cool, but not right now. I need to get to the feed store to help my mom." Small white lie, but he had to stall to gather his thoughts. "I was on my way there when I saw Harley." At least that part was true.

She glanced from the dog to him as if she were trying to discern the truth. "We could do something a little less formal, if that would make you more comfortable. How about tonight? I could make you dinner at my place."

He almost laughed at the look on her face as if she couldn't believe she just asked him to dinner.

"If food is involved, I'm there. If you're sure?"

She nodded. "How about seven-thirty?"

"See ya then." He stood.

"Don't you need the address?"

He chuckled. "The house is where the old Gladstone farm used to be, right?"

"Yes. It overlooks the lake."

"Trust me. I know that area very well." More than once, he and his friends had thrown a party at the old barn, which had been torn down years ago.

"Do you need help with the dog?"

"No, I'm going to go grab my laptop and work here so she can rest. I have a feeling she'll follow those toys wherever I take them."

"Okay, see ya later." He patted the dog and walked out the front door.

He had a date. Well, it was technically an interview, but he was practiced at giving nonanswers. He'd done it his entire military career. All of his assignments were classified, so he couldn't share anything.

Hope she won't be too mad when she finds out I'm as tight-lipped as the rest of Tranquil Waters.

He started the truck engine. The last thing he wanted was the sleepy angel mad at him.

"WHAT WAS I thinking?" Macy blurted into the phone. "You don't invite people you're interviewing to dinner."

"Yes, you do. It's just the dinner's at a restaurant most of the time," her friend Cherie chimed in. "Chill, girl. You're going to have a heart attack. This guy must be superhot to make you so nervous."

Macy slipped on a pair of flats. After his comment about the heels, she realized she'd been trying too hard. Except for those over sixty, this was more of a jeans and T-shirt town. She was perfectly comfortable in that attire.

It wasn't until her breakup with Garrison that Cherie, her nearest and dearest friend, forced her to leave Boston and took her for a makeover in Manhattan. They tossed out everything she'd owned and decided to start fresh with a sexy new wardrobe. Add a brand-new haircut that was perfect for her shoulder-length curls. And a newfound passion for accessories. Cherie had convinced her that shoes and purses were really works of art.

She didn't have to twist Macy's arm very hard.

But if Macy wanted to fit into the landscape of Tranquil Waters, she'd have to scale back on the big-city wardrobe, etc.

"*Superhot* doesn't cover it," she said honestly. "*Scorching* might come close. He puts that gorgeous action-adventure star Tom Diamond to shame."

"Wait. Hotter than Tom Diamond? The man who will be my husband someday, even if I have to shoot him with a tranq gun and stuff him in my trunk? I think it might be time for me to visit Texas."

"You are welcome anytime. I certainly have the room. And yes he's that handsome, and he's sweet to dogs and loves his mother. You know how tough that is for me. He's like a triple threat. But I have to keep this professional. The last thing I need in this gossip-hungry town is to date its hero."

"So you want to date him. Hmm."

"Stop analyzing me and putting words in my mouth," Macy complained. Cherie never stopped being a psychiatrist, but it was her only vice so Macy put up with her.

"You said the words. I'm just placing them in the proper order for you."

"Privacy is impossible at any of the restaurants in town. I'm sure that's why I came up with making the dinner. I wanted him to feel comfortable, to share as much as possible."

"He's a war hero, you know there's not much he can say," her friend warned.

"This isn't my first time." She'd been to almost every war zone in the world the past five years. It had only been the past twelve months that she'd decided to take a permanent position out of the line of fire. Little did she know it was just as dangerous at home.

She'd been shot at, kidnapped twice by insurgents and lost in the middle of the desert. None of that had been as bad as her ex's betrayal.

"Stop thinking about that jerk. He's not worth it."

"How did you know?" Macy laughed at her friend's incredible insight.

"He called here looking for you again. For a hot-shot newspaper publisher, he's not very good at finding people."

Macy snorted. He was one of the best reporters ever, and if he truly wanted to find her, he would. But she'd told him if he did, she'd only turn him away again. It was the truth.

"Of course, I told him to stuff it up his—"

Lights flashed across her bedroom window. "Oh, man, he's here early. Darn those marines and their punctuality."

Macy stared down at the melee of clothing on her bed and picked up the frilly black blouse on top.

"Put down the black, and choose the red. Men love red."

"That was scary. Fine. Red it is. I love you and I wish you'd come see me. It's a nice town but—I still feel very outsiderish."

"Oh, girl, don't you worry. They'll love you as much as I do. Just give them some time and the chance to get to know you. Charm the pants off that marine. That will be a great start."

The doorbell rang and Harley barked twice.

The big dog had settled in just fine. Macy had even bought the dog her own couch for the family room. The fence had been finished that afternoon, and they'd reinforced the gate with two different kinds of locks.

She turned off the phone.

Harley sat patiently at the door waiting for their guest.

Shoving her curls out of her face, Macy took a deep breath and turned the knob.

Oh, shoot, the man is beautiful.

Dressed in dark jeans, cowboy boots and a dark blue button-down under a leather jacket, he was way beyond scorching.

Her normally agile mind couldn't think of the word, but she knew there was one.

This is work. This is work. This is work.

He cocked his head and stared down at Harley.

"Did she run away again?"

"What?" Macy forced her hand to stay still even though she wanted to wave it in front of her own face, which was suddenly too warm even though the temperature outside was in the low fifties.

"Harley? You know the dog?"

He smiled at her as if he were humoring her.

"Uh, sorry. I'd been on the phone and I'm a little—uh—" *Hot for you.* No, that wasn't right. "Out of sorts. Please come in. And Harley lives with me now. She would have been in here days ago, but the rain kept the ground too wet for them to finish putting the fence in."

He handed her a colorful bouquet of chrysanthemums in a vase. "These are a present for your new home." In his other hand he held a large paper bag. "I didn't know what you were cooking so I brought a couple bottles of wine, some dark beer and, er… green tea."

She took the flowers and led him to the kitchen. "Thank you, these are beautiful, but you didn't have to bring anything."

He shrugged and sat the bag down on her quartz countertop. "It's the south, if you don't bring a house-warming gift on the first occasion you visit, or to any party you're invited to, they'll talk about you for years."

"I'll have to remember that," she said. Not that she'd been invited to anything, but maybe some day.

"I probably should have mentioned my kitchen skills are somewhat limited. But I make a mean beef stew. I put it on earlier today, so it should be ready in a few minutes. And I have bread and salad."

"Sounds good to me. In general, I like food, so it doesn't matter too much what it is. After C-Rats, I can, and have, digested everything from guinea pig in Machu Picchu to some weird toad in Africa. I'm not sure that last one didn't lead to a night of hallucinations."

She laughed. "I'm pretty adventurous when it comes to food, but I've never eaten either of those."

"You get to a point where just about everything really does taste like chicken." He smiled and her heart did a double thump.

Oh, heck, I'm in trouble.

She forced a smile.

"Now I feel like maybe I should have tried for something more exotic." She examined the wine bottles he'd brought. He'd surprised her with his choices. She didn't know much about wine, but neither bottle was cheap. "Do you have a preference?"

"Whatever you want is fine with me. I'll be drinking the tea."

At her quizzical look, he explained. "The docs are weaning me off the painkillers for my leg. It's best if I don't drink as it can create an allergic reaction. Although, me and my buddies at the hospital suspected they only told us that so we don't find out how the painkillers are with alcohol. They deal with a lot of addicted vets there."

"We can't have that. Tea it is. The last thing I need is alcohol. It tends to loosen my tongue, and I'm not the one who needs to do the talking tonight."

She caught the tightening of his lips before he turned away. "I don't mind," he said. "If you want a glass of wine. It won't bother me."

"No," she said lightly. "I've grown fond of tea since moving here. Cracks me up that they drink it iced even in the dead of winter."

"Staple of the South," he said, pulling a large plastic pitcher with a lid out of the bag. "Usually it's black tea. I have this friend from China who told me that green tea has healing properties. It also clears away some of the fogginess from the drugs."

"I've heard that, too." She'd forgotten about his injuries. Except for a small limp, he didn't seem to be in much pain. But she'd met plenty of marines and she knew how tough they were. If he had to take drugs, the injuries were severe. The journalist in her wanted to know specifics, but it would wait.

"Before we eat, would you like to see the house? Actually, most of it is my uncle Todd's taste. But I have a few touches here and there."

"I like the stonework on the outside mixed with the pale brick. It blends into the rocky hills behind the house."

"Yes, that was one of his ideas—for it to blend into the landscape. Though, I think it's kind of fun that he added a Gothic touch with some of the windows and the roof alignment.

"Did you know my uncle? I mean, you've been gone awhile, but before?"

"I didn't know him. I probably heard his name around town, but I wasn't much interested in the newspaper when I was a kid. And some might say I was a little self-absorbed back then. I like to say, I was a teenager."

They laughed.

She took him through the family area where Harley plopped down on her sofa. The television was on

Animal Planet, which seemed to be the dog's favorite along with anything on PBS.

He smiled. "She's made herself at home there."

"Oh, that couch is hers. I even had them put extra down in it and then had that wrapped in plastic and an outdoor fabric. Great Danes have joint and bone aches most of their lives. I wanted Harley to have a soft place to rest. Just a minute, I need to change the channel for her."

Picking up the remote, she set it on one of the PBS *Nova* specials. Harley grunted her agreement.

She'd learned about the dog's television preferences earlier in the day when she'd sat with her at her former home. If Macy tried to watch a channel Harley didn't like, the dog would voice her displeasure.

Not that she was spoiled or anything.

The house was a Texas T shape. The various hallways fed into the center area, which was the main entertaining space. "Down that hall are two bedrooms. There's another guest bedroom down that hall—" she pointed "—and the master bedroom and study are down that hall," she said.

It didn't seem appropriate to take him to the bedrooms. "There's a loft upstairs with two more bedrooms. But it isn't really worth the trip up. Let me show you the study. There are a lot of Civil War antiques in there. My uncle was a collector." The rest of the house had been furnished in rich warm tone-on-tone colors. It was a comfortable place to relax at the end of the day. The only room that was slightly feminine was the master bedroom and bathroom, which Macy had decorated.

Macy opened the door to the study and smiled when Blake muttered, "Woooee. This is a museum."

His eyes traveled over the glass cases filled with small items and guns from various Civil War battles.

She'd had the estate appraised and this room alone was worth a couple of million. The study had been outfitted with special equipment that would protect it from fire and anything else Mother Nature might throw at it. The whole house was a bunker of sorts, concrete surrounded by stone. The windows could withstand an F-5 tornado. That was good because in this part of the country hurricanes and tornados happened at least once or twice a year.

"I don't have the heart to auction off these things. Other than the newspaper, this was my uncle Todd's only passion. I can feel his spirit in here, and I just can't let go of his stuff."

Blake blew out a whistle. "I'm no expert, but even I know this is one incredible collection. There are people who'd pay big money for it, but I understand how you feel. My dad collected baseball caps and cards. We still have an entire wall of his hats, some are from teams that no longer exist, and a few are hats his dad had given to him. There's an original Yankees cap in the bunch, but my mom hides that one when her friends come over.

"It was never even a question if we'd keep them. And I feel the same way about them, as you do."

She smiled. "Sounds like you really loved your dad."

Flipping off the light switch, he followed her out the door and to the kitchen.

"Has the interview started?" His voice had changed and he sounded as if he suspected her of trying to get him to talk about his past.

"No. Mere curiosity. I thought I'd feed you before grilling you." She winked at him.

"Then, yes. My dad was a hero to my brother and me. He's the reason I went into the military, albeit he was air force. He was a pilot until he decided to retire and help Mom with the feed store. He was a tough old goat, and my brother and I didn't get away with much when we were kids."

"I met your mom when I first arrived. I had to get a lawn mower and other gardening tools."

He chuckled.

She served up the bowls of stew. "Your mother found me frowning as I checked out the lawn mowers. She dug around in her pockets and handed me a card that had the number of a teenager who does yards. Her exact words were, 'He's a good kid. For four acres it'll be about a hundred dollars a week. If he tries to charge you more, tell him I'll knock him upside the head.'"

Blake laughed. "Yep, that's my mom."

"I loved her. She was one of the few people who was genuinely kind to me. I'd heard Texans are a friendly bunch. And, okay, everyone has been nice to my face. But I get the strangest looks. And as I mentioned earlier, they haven't been exactly welcoming."

He carried both of the bowls to the other end of the counter where there were stools and place settings. "Like I said earlier, soon someone will move to town and then you'll be one of the gang. Just give them more time."

She smiled. "My friend Cherie told me the same thing. I'm not sure why it bothers me so much. I never knew any of my neighbors when I lived in New York, Paris or anywhere in the Middle East. Most of the time I lived out of hotels."

At the mention of hotels, his jaw tightened. She'd read what she could find on him, and knew that he'd been in Africa when he sustained his injuries. He was protecting a visiting American ambassador there. He and most of his men were hit by enemy fire, but they'd saved the ambassador and other dignitaries that day. The soldiers had earned Purple Hearts.

"Don't be too worried about it," he interrupted her thoughts. "Small-town life isn't always what it's cracked up to be. Eventually, you feel like a part of the community when everyone knows your name. It can be a wonderful thing, or a curse." His eyebrow rose.

"A curse?" It hadn't been that bad.

"Oh, yes. And especially if a certain high school girl's dad finds you in the barn with her, um, counting hay straws. He calls your dad, who gives you the I'm-disappointed look in front of the entire town when he finds you later at Lucky Chicken Burger sharing a box with your friends." He looked to the heavens. "People still talk about how he watched as my mom dragged me out by my ear. One of the most embarrassing days of my life."

She nearly sputtered her stew, she laughed so hard. "I can't imagine your mother doing that. She talks so highly of you. She's so proud."

"Now she is. That day, not so much. I was grounded for six weeks after that and wasn't allowed to go on dates alone with a girl until I left for college. If we didn't go in a group, I wasn't given permission to go. I had to write letters of apology to the girl, her parents, my parents and our minister."

He shook his head as she started to laugh again. "Sure, it sounds funny, but back then—my friends and my brother never let me forget it. I ran away to college so fast, it was no joke. Joined the marines to help pay for my bachelors and MBA.

"I was determined I would never come back to this place, but I'm a mama's boy. I probably shouldn't admit that. I missed her and dad so much by the end of that first semester, I hitched a thousand miles to get home by Christmas Eve. Of course, my mom read me the riot act because I could have been killed on the road."

"Still, I bet she was glad to see you."

He nodded. "It wasn't long after that my dad got sick. So I was grateful we had that Christmas together."

A chunk of carrot caught in her throat as she watched the memories pass across his face. There'd been a deep family love there. She envied him that. He grew silent.

She swallowed and had a drink of tea. "My parents traveled a lot for their jobs. We didn't get to have many holidays together. I kind of envy you that."

"What did they do?"

"Journalists. My mom wrote for magazines, my dad was on air for different TV affiliates."

"Are they still at it?"

Macy bit her lip. "No. They were killed in a small-plane crash on their way to report on a new orphanage in India. Happened about eight years ago. Uncle Todd was my last living relative. It's just me now."

Blake frowned. "Sorry. I didn't mean to bring up such painful memories."

She patted his arm. Her fingers tingled from the contact. "You didn't. We were talking about family. I just wish I had what you had and have with your mom. I believe the world would be a better place if more parents were like yours.

"I'm lucky that I have great friends all over the world. They helped me when I lost my parents. I was doing an internship in Bosnia with a newspaper and the military guys I'd been following arranged for me to get a flight home on one of their transports. One of them even flew with me and stayed until Uncle Todd could get to the base. I never forgot that. Kevin Donaldson was his name. He had two kids and a wife who adored him. Anytime I was stateside, they insisted on me coming to visit.

"Wow. Look at me telling you my whole life story. Who is interviewing whom, here? I never talk to anyone like this."

He winked at her. "It's the green tea. Has mystical properties in it."

They both laughed.

"Do you want another bowl?"

"Sure. The stew is good. I miss home cooking."

She handed him another full bowl and shoved the plate of French bread at him so he could reach it. "I—I did some digging. As I mentioned, I've covered the military for years for various assignments. I know you can't tell me exactly what happened, although I do know about the ambassador. That's a matter of public record. And that you guys saved him and the others who were investigating the ammunitions camp someone had discovered in the Congo."

"You have done your research." His voice was guarded again.

"I don't want to ask you anything I know you can't answer. What I would like to know is how it happened. Several of your men were hit, but luckily everyone survived."

He sat his spoon in the bowl and stared down at it.

"Some were luckier than others," he whispered.

Her brow furrowed. "Do you mean the injuries?"

"Yes, and the nightmares. Some of us are having a tough time letting go what happened there."

"What did happen?"

His deep brown gaze cut to her. "You know I can't give you details."

She sighed. "Was it an ambush? From what I've figured out so far, you guys had a peaceful week there until you were getting ready to leave. Then all hell broke loose."

As if Harley had sensed the tension, she nudged between them and put her head on his thigh.

He sucked in a breath.

"Is she hurting you?"

"No. It's just sore, like a bruise. Mind you, her head is like a ton of bricks."

"It is very large. She accidentally bumped my nose earlier with her head when I put food in her bowl, and I thought for sure I'd have black eyes."

He smiled, but it was weak.

Stupid. As professional as she was, it bothered her to realize she'd triggered such old memories—hurtful ones from the look of concern on his face.

That was it. He wasn't just a hero. He was a man. That would be her story. No one needed to read about his nightmares of that terrible day, or the darkness that clearly haunted him. How often had she told that story? Heroes deserved to be recognized, but maybe she could focus on who they were after they came home, rather than who they were then.

So many soldiers were affected by the experiences they'd gone through. Some—not in a good way. But some said that it made them more aware of how small the world could be.

"I have chocolate chip cookies for dessert. Actually, I was going to show you the best way to eat them."

"Well, I thought you ate cookies with your mouth." He gave her an odd look, and she rolled her eyes.

"Ah, where is your sense of food adventure? In fact, I'm going to take that adventuresome nature of yours to a whole new level."

"Bring it on, Macy. I can take whatever you've got."

The seductive, whiskey sound of his voice and his choice of words did all kinds of naughty things to her.

Be careful.

But it was too late. She'd already crossed the line with Lieutenant Blake Michaels, and she wasn't at all upset about it.

3

BLAKE TOSSED AND turned in his bed. Thoughts of Macy in those jeans and that lacy red top made it impossible for him to sleep. He'd wanted to kiss her as soon as he saw her lick the whip cream from her lips. That pink tongue had darted out and all he could think of was capturing it with his mouth. He'd wanted to cover her in the white confection and lick every inch of her.

Damn. He had it bad for her.

He sat up on the side of the bed. He needed a shower, a cold one.

Why did she have to be a reporter? If she had any other occupation he'd be doing his best to get in her bed. He couldn't remember when a woman had affected him the way she did. Her laugh, smile and the way she walked with those lovely curvy hips swaying back and forth held his attention.

He thought back over their conversation. Even though she'd pried, she did it respectfully. True to her word, she hadn't asked him a single thing he couldn't answer. And when she dug a little too deep, she'd backed off and made them chocolate chip cookie pies, her version of the whoopie pie.

She was hot. Smart and funny. The perfect combo.

But he couldn't risk hanging out with a woman who might reveal secrets he prided himself on keeping. He might slip up, get carried away. And the last thing he needed was for his superiors to see something like that in the newspaper.

He'd been thinking about taking the honorable discharge on offer, and maybe settling down like his friends Rafe and Will. They'd all met when Will was their captain on missions in Iraq and Afghanistan.

Will had retired and Rafe had been in charge the day of the ambush. Rafe had all points covered. There was no way they could have anticipated the assault. There would have been a lot more casualties if they hadn't been so prepared.

Before the memories pulled him into the darkness, Macy's smile flashed before him.

Damn. Damn. Damn.

He needed to go for a run, but the docs said it would be another three weeks before his leg could take the pounding.

The town might be small, but they did have a health club that was open twenty-hour hours, specifically for folks who worked shifts.

Grabbing his swim shorts, he pulled on a pair of jeans and a T-shirt. Throwing on his leather jacket, he was at the club in less than five minutes. A swim would be the only thing to burn off the excess energy. It was his substitute form of meditation since he couldn't run. The club was nearly empty at four in the morning, and for that he was grateful. He didn't have to make conversation or smile. The sleepy girl at the desk waved him by when he flashed his membership card.

Diving into the water he struck out hard, his arms and legs going at a blistering pace. After twenty or so laps, he slowed down and cleared his mind. The blank slate, his therapist suggested to calm his nerves, was hard for him to find some days. Tabula rasa, she'd called it. It was a challenge to find it when the sexy woman's face kept popping up over and over again.

Then there was his mother who had waited up to pepper him with questions when he'd returned the night before. Macy had nothing on his mom, who kept giving him strange looks and then smiled when he said he was tired and needed to sleep.

He'd never understood women, and his mom was the most confusing of them all.

"I don't know what that water ever did to you, but I hope you're never that mad at me." Macy's voice penetrated his concentration. He nearly gulped a mouthful of water as he stopped abruptly. He was at the end of a lap, and she stood above the lane in a formfitting navy swimsuit.

Hell. The woman was trying to kill him.

His cock was so hard it hurt. He leaned up against the wall and put his arms on the side of the pool to hide the evidence.

What was he, twelve?

Get yourself under control, Marine.

"I have to give up running for a few more weeks and this is the way I meditate."

She chewed on her lip. "I thought you did yoga, or sat and chanted to mediate."

He smirked. "That's awful closed-minded for someone who has traveled the world. Some people do. But I have trouble shutting off my brain if I'm not moving. When I sit still— Well. I have insomnia and sometimes exercise is the only way I can get myself to calm down."

She sat down and dangled her legs in the water. "I hope it's not because of what we talked about last night," she said worriedly. "It's my nature to push at people until they give me what I want. I tried not to do that with you, but sometimes I just can't help myself."

He couldn't tell her the truth, so he lied. "No, it wasn't that. Well, maybe a little. But not in the way you think." He'd made a fool of himself. "Why are you here?"

She pointed through the window where a man had Harley on a treadmill. "One of the trainers from the rescue shelter is working with Harley. The treadmill is made for people who have bad joints."

"She didn't seem to have any trouble running around the other day."

"No, but she shouldn't have done it. Running like that is bad for her. We're trying to teach her to walk at a fast pace on the treadmill. This was the only time Jack could do it. He's a vet tech at the shelter and his shift starts at seven.

"I thought while they worked out, I'd come do some laps. I didn't realize it was you until you made that last turn. I guess, though I never thought of it that way, swimming is my meditation, too. I do it more to make the puzzle pieces of my life and the stories I tell fit together. When I'm doing something physical, it helps me figure stuff out. And like Harley, I have a bad knee. I like running, but it doesn't like me."

He glanced at her left knee, there was a round puckered scar there, and then a long line that intersected it. His head snapped up, his eyes met hers. "You were hit."

She nodded. "About three years ago. It was a through-and-through, but did some ligament damage on the way out. Nothing like what you've experienced."

The thought of her being harmed brought out his protective instincts. He pulled himself up out of the water and sat beside her. "You don't have a limp."

"Nah. I had some great physical therapists." She traced the scar on his right leg. "Wow, that's nasty. Must really hurt."

Her touch had an instant affect on him. Thankfully her eyes were fixed on his right leg and knee. The scars went from his midthigh through his knee and calf. In all he'd taken three bullets in the one leg. And another one in his back. "It's a lot better than it was six weeks ago. What were you doing when you got hurt?"

"Researching a feature on the Arab spring. A demonstration I was covering got out of hand. Had to run for the border the first chance I got, and we were attacked. We were lucky that the marines were waiting on the other side.

"I got hit. They fired back. Luckily a navy surgeon fixed me up right away and then sent me to a good surgeon and physical therapist in Florida where he had a practice."

"You shouldn't have put yourself in danger like that." The words had more of a bite than he'd meant them to. "You could have been killed."

She pulled her fingers away from his leg as if he'd shocked her. "Uh, it's my job to report the tough stories. And trust me, I've been through worse."

Lifting her curls, she pointed to an ugly scar on the back of her neck.

The air left his lungs.

"That was the one that really scared me." She stared at the water.

He reached out and touched the wound.

She jerked away. "But that's a story for another day. I need to get my workout in. I'm sorry I interrupted yours." She stood and he noticed her toenails were painted a violet color. Something about that made him smile. Then he remembered what he'd done.

"Sorry I touched you. I can't stand violence against women. It—It's one of my triggers."

"Triggers for what?"

"A story for another day," he repeated the phrase back to her. Then he grabbed a towel and wrapped it around his waist. "Have a good swim."

4

WHEN BLAKE TOUCHED Macy it was all she could do not to wrap her arms around him. No one had ever looked at her so tenderly or been so concerned. Her ex had been the one who sent her out on some of her roughest assignments. He'd expected her to be able to handle herself, and she did. But there was a small part of her that wished he'd worried about her once in a while. She should have known something was wrong when she called to tell him that she'd been shot and all he'd worried about was how she was going to get him the story.

She'd made the surgeon wait an hour so she could pound out ten pages and email it to the paper.

Blake would have been frantic worrying about her.

Hey, you are not turning into one of those women.

She refused to be the type of woman who needed the man in her life to save her. Macy prided herself on her independence.

Jumping into lane five, she sluiced through the water. When she thought of the marine, she tried to focus on the story she wanted to tell. But it was complicated. She didn't quite have all the pieces yet. She needed to talk to his mother and others who knew Blake. Well, duh, the whole town knew him.

She wanted a different perspective.

The idea was just out of her grasp. She pushed herself harder and harder until ten laps later she was out of breath and hanging on to the edge of the pool in the same way Blake had earlier.

She glanced through the window to see how Harley was doing. Jack gave her double thumbs-up and she smiled.

Why couldn't she go for a guy like Jack or even his boss, Josh? They weren't the subjects of a story and, as far as she knew, they didn't have any battle scars. Though, she sometimes wondered about Josh. He'd been wounded in some way. It was that haunted look in his eyes.

No one knew better than she did how those scars and secrets could weigh a soul down.

The treadmill slowed, and Jack gave Harley a treat. Climbing the ladder out of the pool, she dressed quickly.

Professional ethics kept her from loading Harley into her car and driving straight to Blake's house. She wanted to comfort him. To hold him in her arms and maybe even slip her legs around him and absorb some of the pain he'd experienced.

When would she realize, she never did simple.

After drying Harley off with a towel, she got her settled in the SUV without any fuss. The dog was too tired to fight her. She lay across the backseat looking exhausted.

As Macy pulled up the long drive to her house, she quickly slammed on the brakes.

Harley growled at her.

The marine plaguing her thoughts sat on the tailgate of his truck more handsome than any man had the right to be.

What was going on?

Her body heated. One glance in the rearview and her cheeks were the color of primroses on a bright sunny day.

Every cell in her body screamed at her. She needed him just as much as he might need her.

Oh.

Cherie would start charging her by the hour.

But before she called her friend, she had to find out why the Blake was here in her driveway. His expression said the weight of the world was resting on his shoulders.

She let Harley out of the backseat.

"Hey," she said as the dog ran up to Blake. He bent over and rubbed the animal's ears.

Macy tried her best not to be jealous, but it wasn't easy.

One small touch from Blake, and she already craved more.

"Hey," he said eyeing her warily. "Sorry I just showed up. We need to talk."

"About?"

"The fact that I touched you without your permission. I was taught better than that. I can write you a letter of apology if you'd like, but I thought it might mean more if I said it in person."

She laughed. "Letters are so old-school. You could have texted me."

He shrugged. "I kind of like the old-school ways, besides, I didn't have your number. And there's something else."

"What's that?"

"I really want to kiss you."

She was in big, big trouble, she could confirm, because she wanted that, too.

"Wow. For a marine, you really aren't afraid to tell it like it is." Macy gave him a smile that didn't quite meet her eyes. He'd made her uncomfortable, but he had to speak his mind. If she told him off, so be it, but he had to let her know how he felt.

If he'd learned anything the past six months, it was that life was short. And from his therapist, that the truth was important.

"It's true. It's who I am. And I understand you and I can't— Well, that is, you have ethics. Some journalists don't anymore, but I can see that you do. We have a connection. I'm fairly certain you've noticed it."

She nodded.

Good, at least the attraction wasn't one-sided.

"But you're writing a story about me and that's a conflict of interest."

"Yes, it is."

"So, I think I have a solution."

She sat next to him on the tailgate and petted Harley.

"Don't write the story."

Immediately her back stiffened. "I can't do that."

"Why not? You're the publisher of the paper, right? Your uncle left you the whole thing, so you make the decisions. Or you could have someone else write the story, though, I'm going to be honest—I wouldn't trust anyone else."

She sighed. "Why do you have to be so—you."

He chuckled. "I'm not sure what that means, but do you agree with me?"

"The story is already compromised because you do strange things to me, Lieutenant Michaels."

He lifted her chin with his fingers and waited. She nodded her approval.

"Strange things?"

"Yes," she said softly. "I always seem to be too warm when you're around."

"Hmm. Maybe you have a fever." He held the back of his hand to her forehead. Then let his fingers trail down her cheek. He leaned in to kiss her.

Harley let loose with a harsh bark.

They broke apart chuckling.

A giant head was eye level with them. Harley's paws were up on the tailgate, and she gave them a look that said break it up.

"I think she's hungry," Macy suggested. "I should feed her."

The dog grumbled.

"Do you mind if I help?"

Macy pursed her lips.

"Hands off, I promise. I won't touch you again until you ask me."

"This isn't a good idea," she said.

"What? Feeding your dog? Surely she would disagree."

Since Macy didn't tell him to leave, he followed her into the house. Keeping his distance so she wouldn't feel pressured.

She needed time to get used to the idea. Hell, they'd only met a couple of days ago and here he was trying to kiss her.

He remembered about the ex. Maybe that wasn't over.

She winced. "I'm trying to fit in and I don't think dating the town hero will help my case."

"See, that's where you have it wrong. I could be just what you need to ingratiate yourself to the town. If I approve of you, well, it doesn't look so good on them if they don't accept you."

She placed the dog's water dish on a raised stand where Harley was mowing through her food. "I'll think about it."

He winked at her. "You do that. I'll pick you up at seven to take you out to eat."

"No," she said. "I mean it. I'll think about it. It hasn't been that long since I got out of a bad relationship. I'm not ready to date yet."

He shrugged. "Who said anything about a relationship? We're sharing a meal. We won't call it a date. We'll call it a mutual companion outing. Besides, you'd be doing me a favor. All the gray hairs keep throwing their daughters at me. You can be my shield."

That made her laugh. "I'm pretty sure you can

defend yourself just fine, Lieutenant Michaels. You don't need me."

He smiled. "But we had dinner last night. Why can't we do it again?"

"Last night it was about work. And frankly, I don't think it's a good idea to leave Harley alone while she's getting used to her new surroundings. I plan on taking her to the office with me so she doesn't feel abandoned."

Rubbing his chin, Blake eyed the dog. "If I can solve the problem with Harley, will you go to dinner with me?"

She bit her lip. He really loved when she did that.

"I'm not sure how many times I can say this isn't a good idea."

"Fine. I agree. It's not a good idea, but I'm having trouble focusing because I keep wondering what it would be like to kiss you. To hold your hand in mine."

"And spending time with me is going to solve that dilemma?"

"Maybe we'll get lucky and you'll bore me to tears. Or I'll be allergic to your perfume. You might like a movie I despise. I'm kind of a movie snob." That last bit was true. In college, he'd refused to date any woman who hadn't seen his two favorite films, *To Kill a Mockingbird* and *North by Northwest,* they were now followed closely by *Zero Dark Thirty.*

Movies were his favorite escape, and he took them seriously.

Shoving her curls behind her ears she stared at him.

"So, I'd really be doing you a favor by sharing

a meal at this mutual companion outing? We'll get bored with each other and then we can move on, right?"

"Exactly," he told her, but he didn't believe it for a minute. She was bright, funny and beautiful. A triple threat as far as he was concerned. Blake didn't want to think about the future. For now he just wanted the clever journalist with the curvy hips any way she'd take him.

5

AMANDA PELEGRINE, the receptionist at *Tranquil Waters News,* put down her nail file and eyed Macy warily. For once, Harley was on her best behavior and strode in as if she owned the place. Macy was certain it had nothing to do with the giant box of dog treats and sack of brand-new toys she had in her hand.

Amanda, who was not Macy's biggest fan, sneered. "I'm allergic to dogs."

Good. Maybe you'll quit.

She'd wanted to fire the useless female since the day she took over the paper. But her uncle's will stated she had to wait three months before making any staffing changes.

He'd left her with an angry receptionist, who looked like something from the circus with her fuzzy raspberry sweater, two-inch-long green nails and fascinator that looked like a dead bird on a perch.

Having lived in big cities, Macy was used to all kinds of fashions, but she'd never seen someone like Amanda.

In addition to the snarky witch, she had one reporter, Darla, who was amazing, but eight month's pregnant with her second child.

The only columnist was Hugo, who was eighty, possibly ninety. Old enough that he couldn't remember what year he was born. He couldn't hear or see, but the man could write. He used an old manual typewriter, which meant someone else had to scan his stories into a computer.

Twice a week Macy stopped by to pick up his columns. She always had to make sure she scheduled an extra hour for each visit because Hugo was just as good at telling a story as he was at writing one.

He'd seen so much, and she enjoyed listening to him talk about the good old days.

"Well, Amanda, she'll be coming here with me every day. I'm happy to give you a severance package, otherwise, I suggest you invest in some antihistamines."

"Maybe I'll just talk to my friend the lawyer about working conditions." Her heavily colored eyebrow rose into her bangs. She wore so much makeup it was impossible to tell her age.

If Macy had to wager a guess, it would be somewhere around twenty-seven, but that was debatable.

She hadn't meant to sound rude, but she'd grown weary of the woman's constant negativity. "You do that." She only had to wait one more week before giving her the heave-ho.

"No reason to get testy. By the way, you have some messages." She stuck out her hand with a pile of pink notes.

"It's only nine in the morning."

The woman shrugged. "Some might be from the last couple of days. I cleaned off my desk when I was looking for my good nail file and I found them."

Stuffing the messages in her pocket, Macy's mouth formed a thin line. "In my office in fifteen minutes," she said through gritted teeth.

"But I have a—"

"Amanda, my office in fifteen," she said harshly as she entered her office. She slammed the door.

Harley whined.

"Sorry, old girl, but she is too much." Rolling out a furry mat that had gel on the underside, she put it behind her desk. Then she added a stuffed toy along with one of the chewies she'd bought at the discount store just outside of town.

Lucky for her, Great Danes were notoriously lazy. Once the dog was comfortable, she'd probably sleep most of the day.

Macy's phone rang. "Call from Boston," Amanda said snidely. "Same guy."

"Tell him I'm in a meeting."

She hung up before the receptionist could question her decision.

She had no interest in talking to her ex. The man had tried to apologize countless times. But she'd caught him red-handed, meaning in bed with his intern. Not one to give into hysterics, she'd turned on her heel, picked up her laptop and walked out with only the clothes on her back.

The week before she'd found him cheating, she'd received a visit from her uncle's attorney. At first, she thought she would sell her inheritance and use the proceeds for an amazing honeymoon.

But after what had happened, she decided it was a sign to move in a new direction. She'd been a high-profile, far-flung reporter for a long time. She had the awards and reputation to prove it.

So instead of planning a honeymoon, she gave two weeks' notice at the Boston paper and told HR she was taking two of the six weeks of vacation owed to her. She waited until she knew her ex was in a meeting, and went to the condo and packed up everything she owned.

A gypsy, always on the road, she didn't have much other than her clothes, shoes and a few pieces of art she'd picked up during her travels.

She then bought a car and drove to New York to visit Cherie. After a couple of days of being analyzed by her best bud, she knew her choice to move to Texas was a great one.

As soon as she saw her uncle's house, it felt like home, a feeling she hadn't experienced in years. It had surprised her how easy it'd been to walk away from the life she'd thought she wanted and the man she was supposed to marry. That was when she'd known—the obvious reason aside—he wasn't Mr. Right, after all.

Still, she had no desire to speak to him.

A knock on the door interrupted her revisiting the past.

"Come in."

Harley raised her head to see who entered and then lay back down. Amanda stood in the doorway.

"Have a seat." Macy pointed to the chair.

Eyeing her warily, she sat.

"As you know, the three months are almost up. I wanted to give you notice now so that you have time to find another job." Macy picked up a folder. "This is the severance package my uncle had in his files. I will honor it, even though—" She'd been about to say, "you don't deserve it." She shoved the folder across the desk.

"You're firing me?" Amanda's face crumbled. Huge black mascara tears dripped down her cheeks. "I knew it. Why don't you like me?"

Seriously?

"You've been hostile to me ever since I arrived. The missing messages today are just one in a long line of problems with you being inept at your job."

A good manager would have found a way to cushion the blow, but Macy was at the end of her patience with the woman.

"It is nothing personal. It's business. I need to employ people who are efficient and can carry extra duties when necessary. I can barely get you to answer the phone, and that's your only job. I've had to do all the admin, customer service and deal with circulation. That's on top of writing, editing and publishing the paper."

The woman sniffled.

Closing her eyes, Macy gathered her thoughts.

"I—thought you were going to get bored fast and hire someone to take over, so I didn't think it was worth getting to know you or impress you," Amanda said finally. "And you never asked me to do those things. You told me to answer the phone, so I did. I noticed the second week you were here that the accounts receivables were a mess, so I've been doing those. It takes me a little longer than it took Todd, but he'd been doing it for years. And I sort of had to teach myself those first few weeks. You never even said thank-you."

Her eyes popped open. "What?"

"That I was doing so much of the accounting. I'm pretty sure I've done it right, but you might want to have an accountant look over the books. My mom was able to help me with some of it, but once the treatments started, well. You should probably have the figures double-checked."

Macy groaned inwardly. She'd assumed her uncle used a firm to monitor the accounts receivable or payable. There was still so much she had to learn.

The first order of business was to find a good accountant to go over those books.

"We all thought you'd sell the paper, or quit and fold it up. So I didn't see any sense in putting forward any extra effort other than the day-to-day stuff until you figured out what you wanted to do.

"And you were so serious and businessy when you arrived. You didn't treat us any differently than the file cabinets, the gray ones you didn't like. I asked those first few days if I could help you with something, but you looked at me like I was a crazy person.

"I know I don't dress as fancy as you do. But clothes are how I express myself. And I've been studying so hard. I hid the books when you walked by because I was afraid you'd get mad if you saw me. I wanted to talk to you about it. I was hoping, since you were a woman, that maybe you'd give me a chance. But you make me so nervous, I don't know if I'm doing anything right and I sure don't want to ask for a favor."

Staring down at the files on her desk, Macy thought back. She'd been off on her own for so long that she was used to doing everything herself. When she was on assignment, it was expected.

And she'd been sullen and angry when she first got to Tranquil Waters. Had she taken it out on the staff? Did she have the scary face, her game face, on as Cherie called it, when she was walking around town? The same face she had when traveling, so that no one bugged her? No wonder folks thought she was some mean, Yankee shrew.

"That doesn't explain your hostility, Amanda, and what do you mean you've been studying hard? I've seldom seen you without a nail file in your hand."

"You know how you don't know how to act so you act like the other person even though you don't know why someone hates you…. I guess that's what happened. When a person is mean to me, I just do the same back. I'm kind of flaky. I'll give you that.

"You're some important war correspondent, I figured being professional maybe meant being mean. I saw that old movie *The Devil Wears Prada*. That editor was horrible."

Was the woman really taking her cues from a film?

"Yes, but that was fiction. I don't expect you to fall all over yourself, but I do insist on common courtesy." She held up the messages. "And this—this is bad."

The woman scrunched her face. "I considered

throwing them in the trash so you wouldn't find out. It took everything I had to give them to you. When you came in yesterday, you were in such a hurry that I didn't get a chance to pass them on. I stuck them under the phone so I'd remember, but Mrs. Dawes, the cleaner, must have moved them."

Macy gave her an incredulous look.

"I know, I know. But I mean it. I've been studying journalism at an online college. I have to do it like that because my mom is sick and I have to be home to watch my brothers at night when my dad's at work. So in the mornings, I'm tired and can barely keep my eyes open. The nail file thing is a kind of way to trick myself. I hate the sound, but it keeps me awake.

"I promise I'll try to be better. I'll do whatever you ask, just give me two more weeks."

Amanda folded her hands in her lap. The tears continued to roll down her face, and each one churned Macy's stomach a little more.

She felt sick. If the story was true, and her instincts said that it was, Macy had indeed been horrible with a capital *H*.

Journalism 101 was to find out the real story. Everyone had one, and most of the time they were fascinating.

"May I ask what's wrong with your mom? And you should know, as an employee, you do not have to tell me."

"Breast cancer. It's her third time with it. My grandma and aunts all died of it. But she's doing better. This last round of chemo and radiation has taken its toll, but the docs say her counts are good. Dad drives her to Houston once a week for treatment.

"She just doesn't have any energy. I'm the oldest of four, and all under sixteen. So I help out around the house and try to give them money when I can, since Mom can't work right now."

Shame on you, Macy Reynolds. Shame on you.

Dear God, she'd almost fired the poor woman and had the entire family out on the street.

The journalist in her told her to stop right there, that she was being too soft. If Amanda worked at one of the top one hundred papers, she'd be out. Everyone had to do the job of five or six people these days. When Macy started out as a reporter, she'd had to turn in only three columns a week. Her last job in Boston, she'd had to do a minimum of eight, and help with copyediting and online coverage.

But the *Tranquil Waters News* was not a top one hundred paper. She was certain it wasn't even ranked, though for a small paper, they had a good circulation.

"I see. That is unfortunate." Her words sounded cold, even to her. But she'd never been great at the touchy-feely stuff. Except when it came to Harley, that dog turned her into a pile of emotional mush.

"So, you've been studying journalism. What year are you?" She forced a smile.

"I'm a junior. I was all set to go to Texas State, but then Mom got sick again, so I enrolled online."

Rummaging through the old desk, Macy found her personnel file. She was only twenty years old.

Holy hell. That explained so much.

But they had to set some ground rules.

"Are you really allergic to dogs?"

The girl glanced at Harley. "No, but I'm scared to death of them. One tried to bite me once when I was a kid and I've never been able to get close to a dog since. I'm sorry, but that's the truth."

Macy nodded. "This one won't hurt you. She is the friendliest dog. Aren't you, Harley."

The dog lifted her head and cocked it sideways. A low grunt of what sounded like her agreement followed.

Amanda laughed.

"She'll hang out with me most days," Macy explained. "So it might be good if you two tried to be friends. I won't force it, but if you're going to make friends with a dog, this is the one to start with. I promise."

"I'll try."

"Okay. Well, if you're staying, we'll need some changes. Ones that you and I will decide on together."

"I'll do whatever you want, no problem." Amanda held up her hand as if she were swearing an oath in court.

"Good. To begin with, you'd better give me the lowdown on my other employees."

Macy listened carefully to each backstory. Amanda knew it all, which showed she had a propensity for getting the truth out of folks. Not a bad trait for a budding journalist.

"I'll come up with a code of conduct and expectations for you to sign off on. And we'll consider the next two weeks as a probation period," Macy said. "If that goes well, we'll extend it.

"As for your wardrobe, I don't want you to feel like you can't express yourself, but I do want to offer you suggestions on proper attire for the office."

Amanda made a weird face. "I don't have any old lady clothes or sexy librarian stuff like you wear," she said. "But I could maybe tone it down a little."

"How about we compromise with one bright color a day? And maybe jeans that don't show more than they should?"

"Fine by me. Would you like me to get you a coffee?"

Hmm. That sounded good. "Tell you what, you like those lattes from the café. Why don't you get one and I'll take a black coffee. Here's some cash. And then, please find out when everyone can come in for a staff meeting. We need to chat."

"That's going to be a bit tough on Hugo, but I can give him a ride from the nursing home if that's okay with him."

"We'll figure it out. I'd also like to talk to the printer, and before you leave today, I need access to those books. I'll hire an accountant this afternoon."

"Got it, Boss!" She hopped up. "Coffee, and then I'll make the calls. Thank you!"

Macy smiled. "You're welcome."

Amanda turned back when she reached the door. "Uh, there's one other thing."

Macy's eyebrow rose, but she didn't say anything.

"I have to write a feature story for one of my classes. I know it's a lot to ask, but if I can find the subject, can you just edit it for me? You know, like a real editor would?"

Someone long ago had done that for Macy, and life really was about karma. "Sure. Just bring it to me when you're ready."

A bright smile lit Amanda's face. "Wow. You really aren't the complete witch we thought you were."

When she shut the door, Macy snorted.

Well, at least there's that.

6

FOR THE PAST two days, a certain newspaper publisher had avoided Blake. She'd claimed that she was too busy with work. He didn't consider it stalking when he'd driven by the newspaper office on the way to the feed store and noticed her car was there.

No. It wasn't stalking.

For the life of him, he didn't understand why he couldn't get her out of his head.

Well, except for the fact that she was sexy as hell, smart and funny when she wanted to be. The waitress at the Lone Star Café had been gossiping about the new lady with the giant dog when he had his breakfast that morning.

"She's so uppity. Have you seen her walking around? That sneer on her face. I want to tell her that she'll catch more bees with honey, but she tips good so I ain't sayin' a darn thing," the waitress said.

Obviously, not everyone saw Macy the way he did. But then, he had heard her story. Orphaned, world traveler who was in search of a home. He knew that last bit because he felt the same way.

He was lucky that he had his mom, and that would always be home. Nevertheless, he was at a crossroads in his life. Again, he was lucky that he had many opportunities open to him. A marine to his core, the idea of desk duty didn't sit well with him. Pushing papers might be great for some folks; he liked to stay active and to be challenged.

There were a couple of business opportunities. He could take over one of the divisions of the security company he'd invested in with Rafe and Will. And his brother, J.T., had mentioned a number of other businesses that were looking to expand into Tranquil Waters. He liked the idea of being in on the ground floor of something and watching it grow.

His phone rang. He didn't recognize the number, but he picked it up.

"Hello."

"Lieutenant Michaels, this is Amanda from the *Tranquil Waters News* calling for Ms. Reynolds. She's in a meeting right now, but she wondered if you might be available to stop by the office either today or tomorrow afternoon."

Ms. Reynolds, eh. "Today is fine. What time?"

"Four-thirty will work well with her schedule."

"Fine by me."

They hung up.

She didn't call him herself, but she wanted to see him. Was she going to pawn his story off on another reporter?

He'd already told her that he wouldn't trust any-one else.

Glancing at the clock, he realized he had about an hour before the meeting.

She had a penchant for sweets. She said it was one of her few vices when she showed him her version of a whoopie pie.

Blake knew exactly what to do.

STANDING IN FRONT of the bathroom mirror at her of-fice, Macy pushed her curls into some semblance of a style and reapplied her lipstick. She tried to convince herself that it wasn't for Blake's benefit.

Liar.

I need to look my best so I can convince him that my new plan for the story is a great one.

She wasn't sure he'd see it that way. Mentally, she prepared counter arguments for many of the points he might bring up.

Her eyelashes, which were much lighter than her hair color, were barely visible. She pulled out the mascara Cherie had insisted she buy on her shopping spree and applied a coat to one eye.

As she did the other, someone knocked on the door. She jabbed the stick into her eye, leaving a trail of black down her cheek.

"Banana shakes." Her least favorite flavor.

"Sorry, but your four-thirty is here. You told me to let you know as soon as he arrived," Amanda said.

"Thanks. I'll be there in just a minute."

Gathering up some tissues, she dabbed at the eye and did her best to remove the black makeup.

Most of it came off, but…that's when she remembered the sales woman telling her that she'd need an oil-based cleanser to remove it entirely.

Wonderful.

Both eyes were red now and watering. Why was it that if you poked one eye, both of them did that? This was useless. She could call out to Amanda and cancel the meeting, but Blake would know she was here.

She had no other choice.

When her nose started running, she did the only thing she could. Tucking a good chunk of toilet paper up her sleeve, she went to the reception area to meet Blake.

Concern etched his face when he saw her. "Did something happen?" He reached out to touch her, but then pulled back.

She remembered what he said about not wanting to touch her until she asked.

"I was going to lie and say allergies, but I'm not so good at lying. I stuck my mascara wand in my eye and now my face has turned into a faucet."

Blake coughed to cover a chuckle. But she knew what he'd done, and she smiled.

"Yes, I am beauty and grace." She curtsied.

"Do you want to postpone the meeting?" he asked.

"I'm okay, as long as you don't mind my weepy face."

"That face is beautiful no matter what is going on."

"Such a flatterer. I bet you say that to all the women."

"No, only one woman." He said it so low, she wasn't sure she heard him right.

Clearing her throat, she motioned to the chair across from her desk. She'd cleaned out all the file cabinets that had crowded the space and moved the heavy, carved desk so that it faced the door. She'd painted the dull army green a bright cream and brought in some art. She spent most of her days in the space and she liked that it was comfortable.

He set a box from the café on her desk. Then he pushed it toward her. "These are a peace offering for invading your space the other day. I should have called before I came by."

She grinned. "You surprised me, but I didn't take offense. I'm just not in a space where I can—" She lifted the lid on the box. "You got Mrs. Chesaline to make her éclairs? But she only does that on the second Tuesday of the month. I was waiting at the door last week at 5:00 a.m. when I found out what day she made them."

"I heard." He grinned.

She shook her head and frowned. "This town. I swear everything you do is circumspect."

"Yes, but it has its advantages, as well. When you need a helping hand, it's there. You'll see."

She wasn't so sure about that. It was easy for the handsome marine. The town hero home from the battlefield. Not so much for an uptight reporter who was too nosy for her own good.

"I appreciate you taking the time to come over. I've been tied up in interviews all day."

"Who were you interviewing? That is if you can tell me," he said.

"Oh. Uh. Actually, I'm hiring a couple of reporters. Well, I'm hoping I can find reporters who can also edit and lay out pages. I found an ad salesman, next up I need an accountant."

"Is that why you called?" He leaned forward and she caught his pine scent. It wasn't fair that he was beautiful and smelled so good.

"Excuse me?"

"About the accounting position. I don't practice but I do have my license."

She'd forgotten about him having an MBA. The man was so much more than eye candy, which made him so darn appealing. As if he needed any help.

"Well, you know. If you don't mind consulting until I can find someone for us full-time, that would be appreciated."

He nodded. "I can do that. I have something on for tonight, but I'll take a look tomorrow."

Wait, what kind of plans did he have? Was it a date? Why should it matter to her?

Because you know he wants to kiss you.

They had chemistry. But he was so hot he probably had that with every woman he met. He didn't seem like a player, but her track record wasn't the best when it came to men. She no longer trusted her instincts in that regard.

"Tomorrow. Yes. Listen, I appreciate you stepping in temporarily, but that isn't why I asked you to stop by."

He started to say something, but stopped.

Her eyebrow rose. "Please, go ahead."

"I was hoping you asked me for personal reasons."

She smiled. "I'm afraid you're going to be disappointed. It's about the interview. The one for your story."

He leaned back in his seat and eyed her suspiciously. "Are you doing the interview?"

"Hear me out, please."

Frowning, he stood. "Look, I understand this is what you people do, but I told you. I'm not interested in talking to anyone else."

"Why, because you like me?"

"I do, but it's because I trust you. And I've read your work. Whatever you wrote, it would be fair." His voice had grown raw and deep.

She'd touched a nerve.

"You're right. It would be fair if I did the article. And I'm flattered you know that. But what I have in mind goes far beyond just you. The person is someone you'll trust even more than me."

He crossed his arms. "Who?"

"You."

He huffed. "I'm no writer, and it doesn't make sense for me to do a story on myself. You should know I'm not a big fan of games." He was to the door in three strides.

"Hey, I'm sorry. I didn't explain it well. But I'm not exactly sure what it was I said that set you off."

He didn't turn around, but he didn't open the door.

"I thought it would be interesting if you interviewed other veterans, there are so many at the nursing home and the Lion's Club. Not really about war, but about what it's like to come home. How hard it is for families and friends who weren't there to understand what you've gone through." She stood, but didn't move toward him.

Instead, she continued. "The first time I came home from Afghanistan, I couldn't process what had happened. I tried to pretend like it was another life. But after a year of being stressed about everything, even if I'd ever live to write my next story—" She took a deep breath and pushed the painful memories away.

"I was in the newsroom in Boston. One minute I was packing up to go home and the next I was huddled, shivering at my desk unable to speak.

"My uncle Todd came to the rescue again. He'd covered Desert Storm. He got it. And he's the one who called my friend Cherie, who happens to be a psychiatrist. Between the two of them, I was able to talk about it.

"And Cherie taught me coping mechanisms. So thankfully I was able to go back. I had to go back. A lot of important stories needed telling. You get why I had to go back? You've done it time and again yourself, but many people don't. But what we don't always realize is that it not only takes a toll on us—you and I—it takes a toll on our family and our friends."

As he turned to face her, a myriad of emotions passed over his face. His knuckles turned white as he gripped the back of the chair he'd been sitting in. She didn't worry, though, and she certainly didn't fear him. This was his way of channeling anger.

"Being overseas in such conditions—it changes us, Blake. Sometimes for the better, other times not. As much as I'm a loner, I'm a lot more compassionate than I ever was. A journalist must be objective, but even I had to examine my life when I got home again."

She took her seat and gestured for him to take his. "I want to tell you something off the record. Something no one, except Cherie, has heard me say. I'm telling you because I know I can trust you."

"You can trust me," he said gruffly.

Why did she feel the need to confess? She didn't talk to anyone like this.

He sat in his chair. "You don't have to tell me right now," he said. "I believe you. And I'm sorry I—lost my temper. I'm trying very hard to simplify my life. Get up in the morning, do my job, go to sleep at night. I need that kind of routine right now. Things have to be easy."

"I get that. I suppose it's why I'm a workaholic. It happens to be the one constant in my life. We really are a lot more alike than either of us wants to admit."

A long silence followed before he spoke up. "Your idea for the veterans story and their experiences back home is a great one, but I'm not a writer. And you've been there, anyway. Seems to me you'd be perfect for the job."

"Thanks for that. But they'd still be talking to a reporter. I feel like..." She paused. Frustrated she wound a curl around her finger. "This might be really positive for them. I'll help you write the stories, but you need to be the one to do the interviews. How these men and women learned to assimilate back into society could be important for soldiers who are still coming home."

"They have programs," he said, crossing his legs. "Most branches of the military have a system in place where they work with families and do just that. Assimilate."

"Yes, I know, but how you'd write the story would be completely different. Everyone who comes home deals with it in his or her own way. That's why this will work. Readers will be able to say, 'Hey, that's the way I felt.' Or, 'No wonder my dad spent so much time alone in his study.'"

"It all sounds kind of therapist-like to me," he said.

She knew exactly what he meant. "It would be if I had a psychologist writing the stories. I tell you what, how about you do one or two interviews and see how it goes? If it's not your thing—I won't say another word about it."

Harley grumbled beside her and then made her way around to Blake where she placed her head on his lap. Her stomach made an appalling noise.

"Do you need me to walk her?" Blake asked as he stroked the dog's head.

"No, she only went out an hour or so ago. It's time for her dinner, though, and she gets two *c-o-o-k-i-e-s*." Harley's head popped up and she immediately began to drool on his shoe. "You cannot spell!"

Blake laughed. "I'm not so sure about that. I need to get going. I'll think about what you said. Maybe I'll have an answer for you tomorrow when I come check your books."

"You'll still do that?"

"Said I would, and I always keep my word."

"Thank you. I do appreciate it, and I promise I'll

do my best to find someone to help me on a more permanent basis."

"There's something else you should think about," he said.

"What's that?"

"The story you were about to tell me. I saw that look in your eyes. I know it well. If we eventually do this, you should share your own story with readers. It isn't just the military that is overseas and comes back wounded physically and mentally."

"That's true," she admitted. "But I'm not so sure people would be interested in my story, especially in this town. I'd kind of like to keep my head down low. Maybe at some point, fifty or so years down the road, they'll forget I'm the new girl."

"Like you said, the articles could shed some light on why certain people are the way they are. And how they deal with the day-to-day. I have a feeling if the rest of the town knew about what happened to you, it would change things."

Perhaps. But dredging up old memories was the opposite of what she needed. More than anything, she wanted to start fresh. That was what moving to Tranquil Waters had been all about.

7

"Hon, I hate to do this to you, but I need a big favor," his mother said as he walked in the house. The talk with Macy had him riled up and anxious. He wasn't exactly sure why. That look on her face when she thought back to her time overseas, he'd seen it one too many times in the mirror. It bothered him that she'd suffered so much. He wanted to sooth her, to help her forget.

"Blake?" his mother asked.

"Yes, ma'am, whatever you need." He rounded the kitchen and stopped when he saw her worried expression. She had a small suitcase packed.

"Mom? What's wrong?"

She put her hands on her hips. "Momma D isn't doing so well. Your aunt Eloise wants to put her in a rest home, but Momma isn't very keen on the idea. Right now she's in the hospital, and says all she wants to do is be in her own home. She's insisted that she'll heal better with her things around her and being close to her gardens. Even with the full-time nurse, Eloise thinks it's still too much for her at the moment. So I need to go down to San Antonio and look after her for a bit. See what's up."

"Do you need me to drive you? I can be ready in ten minutes."

She put her palm on his cheek. "You are such a good boy. I hate leaving you so soon after you've just got here, but it can't be helped, I'm afraid. I was hoping you could keep an eye on the store. Ray and Tanya pretty much run the place already, I do the books and talk to folks. You wouldn't have to do much. Make the bank deposits. Give Ray a hand with the inventory. You've done it all before when you were a kid. Nothing has changed, except it's all on computers now."

Well, he'd said he needed purpose and routine. Crazy how the universe worked sometimes. "When I saw Momma D on my way up, she seemed fine."

His mother waved dismissively at him. "She's old and a cold can turn into pneumonia in a heartbeat. But don't you worry about her. She's a tough old broad."

He frowned. "Seems like I'd be better off helping you guys down there than I would be here. Like you said, Ray has a handle on things."

"Oh, no, honey. I'll feel better if you're here. I'm going to sit around and gossip with her. And I'll make sure her gardens are ready for the winter. You know how much I love doing that stuff. She has only the one television, so I imagine we'll sit around watching her programs with the sound blaring."

There was that. When he'd stopped by on his way up to Tranquil Waters, he spent the day with this grandmother. She was his mom's stepmother. Her

mom had died when she was only three, and Momma
D had become the only mother she really knew.

She was nearly deaf, but she didn't miss much.
When he visited her, she was in her parlor, which
was what she called the living room, watching her
afternoon soaps at an earsplitting octave.

But she'd taken one look at him and shaken her
head. "Boy, you need a hug." Then she'd held out
her arms. Damn if she wasn't right. He'd ended up
spending the night there because he loved being in
her presence. She was a positive light, and he needed
that in his life.

"Your brother will be by in an hour. I asked him
to bring you some dinner because I didn't have time
to cook."

"Mom, I'm perfectly capable of taking care of myself. I've been doing it a really long time."

"Don't take a tone with me, son. Besides, I want
you to grill your brother. Mona who works as a teller
at the bank says she could have sworn she saw your
brother in the parking lot, in his truck, with a woman
in there. She had red hair. I never thought your brother
would go for a redhead."

He snorted. In another five minutes, she'd have
J.T. married off with five carrot-orange-haired kids.

"I'll take your bag to the car. Is there anything
else you need?"

She scrunched up her face, and glanced around
the kitchen. "No— Oh, if you don't mind, maybe
you could take the sack of seeds on the workbench
and put it in the car. And there are two rosebushes

by the garage I'm going to take to Momma. They are heirloom, and you know how much she loves them."

It was a bit late in the fall to be planting, but it was San Antonio so the weather stayed pretty warm throughout the year.

Fifteen minutes after she left, his brother rolled up in the driveway in his truck. He didn't bother knocking, just walked through the back door like everyone else in town did. His mom's house was known as a gathering place.

"Stupid jarhead can't even fix a meal on his own." J.T. put a sack from the diner on the kitchen counter. Except for the paint color on the walls, which was a warm yellow, not much had changed in the light-filled kitchen since he was a kid. There were good memories in that kitchen of holiday baking, birthdays and his dad cooking dinner while encouraging Blake and J.T. with their homework. His mom was at the feed store a lot in those early years, so the men in the family had to learn to do for themselves, which wasn't a bad thing.

"Shut it, nerd. Did you bring me a chocolate donut this time?"

The nerd stuck two chocolate donuts on a plate.

"Why didn't you tell Mom you had already planned to come over and watch the game?" The first Mavericks' basketball game of the season started at seven.

"Brownie points, dude. It made me look good to bring dinner to the poor, broken jarhead."

"I'll show you broken if you don't stop calling me jarhead. Come on, nerd, I set up the TV trays in the family room. And thank you again for buying Mom that fifty-six-inch flat screen for Christmas last year. It's the best gift you've ever given her."

They chuckled at that.

"You could have come out to my place," his brother said.

"Not if I want to drink this," he raised one of the two beers he was holding in his hands. Earlier that day he'd visited the local doc for a checkup. He was down to half a pain pill a day. His leg continued to hurt like hell, but it only reminded him that there was still work to do on his body. The doc had given him permission to have one beer, maybe two, a day.

"I have a perfectly fine couch you could sleep on."

He shrugged. Time to have a little fun.

"So Mom says you're getting engaged to some redheaded chick. Who is she?"

J.T.'s beer spewed from his mouth onto his burger. "What the—?"

"Some lady at the bank saw you. Therefore, it must be true." Damn, he'd missed giving J.T. a hard time. The surprise on his brother's face was priceless.

He laughed so hard his gut hurt.

"Sometimes I hate this town," his brother growled. "She's not some chick. Her name is Anne Marie and she's a colleague. We were not on a date. We'd been at a conference in Houston. The rest is none of your business."

Blake held up his hands in surrender. "Hmm. I think he doth protest too much."

"Just watch the game, jarhead."

For the next two hours they did. Screaming at the

refs, who called fouls on everything. It was close but the Mavs won.

They clinked beer bottles.

Blake was relaxed, truly so. He almost felt like a normal human being. He'd been on for so long, he forgot what it was like to let go. Even in the hospital it had been one operation after another and then intense physical therapy.

He took a long breath.

The psychiatrist said he needed time. He understood now. Bit by bit it was coming back to him, how to live a life where he wasn't constantly looking over his shoulder or listening for changes in the wind. He'd never stop being a marine, but he could learn to be calm and enjoy things again. Maybe even sleep more than three hours at a time.

His mind wandered through his conversation with Macy. Could he do what she asked? It might dredge up a lot of issues he didn't want to think about. Then again, sometimes it helped to talk about what happened.

He sipped his second beer.

Then there was his other problem. The one that had kept him awake and unsettled ever since he'd seen her beautiful face in the pouring rain. Never in his life had he felt such a pull toward another person.

It was as if she had an invisible rope tied directly to his heart. He'd met her a couple of days ago, and he—what?

He'd almost lost his temper earlier, and she hadn't backed away one bit. She'd glanced at him, noticed his clenched hands and then looked him straight in the eye.

And she was right. They did have a great deal in common. What would it hurt to date? See her a few times, and get her out of his system. If he wrote the story she asked for, she couldn't use work as an excuse. He wouldn't take any payment for the accounting he'd do, or for writing the article.

So technically she wouldn't be his boss. She'd have to edit the piece, which might give her an out. But he'd find a way around that.

I know what I have to do.

8

THE SUN DIPPED below the lake and the wind gusted. Standing on the back deck of her uncle's place, Macy threw the ball for Harley. The dog loved to run, a little. It wasn't long before Harley kept the ball in her mouth and walked past Macy into the house where she dropped it into her basket of toys.

Chuckling, Macy shut the door and locked it. Using the remote, she turned on the fireplace, and padded to the kitchen to see if her marinara was ready. She'd made the sauce in the slow cooker earlier in the day. Her housekeeper had the next two weeks off while she cared for her ailing grandson, who had chicken pox. From what Macy could discern, the itchy disease had made the rounds of most of the elementary school and a number of day cares. They'd done a small feature about how to care for children and adults with the disease.

Macy didn't mind being on her own. If she had a choice, she'd let the housekeeper go. But she didn't. After setting a pot of water on the stove to boil, she picked up her cell phone to make sure she hadn't missed a call.

His call.

Blake had left a message at the office that he was busy at the feed store. He said he'd let her know when he could come by to do the accounting. It was almost five-thirty and he hadn't contacted her.

He was either really busy, or he might have forgotten.

Why was she disappointed? She'd heard through the Tranquil Waters grapevine that his mother was out of town for some reason.

"Cassidy Lee said she happened to spot Blake out behind the store, loading lumber into a truck." Macy had eavesdropped on the waitress's conversation as she lingered by the register at the café to pay for her lunch. The waitress in question had the rapt attention of a table full of women. "He had his shirt off, and she said it took everything she had not to walk up to him and start licking his abs. It's not a six, it's an eight-pack, ladies. And he has those sexy cut-ins on his hip. I asked her about the scars from his injuries, and she said, 'What scars? I was too distracted by those muscles.'"

The table of women whooped.

"Imagine how hot he must have been to take his shirt off when it's so chilly outside." One of the women fanned her face. "I think I might have to stop by the feed store to pick up some—" she paused for a few seconds "—seeds."

The other women tittered and joked.

Blake was a hot commodity in this town. Most of

the men his age and a little older were for one rea-son or another not available. She'd learned that bit of news from Amanda, who said she went to Austin if she wanted to dance because then she didn't have to worry about some guy's wife giving her a hard time the next day.

While Macy waited for the water to boil, she cleaned up the mess Harley had made around her food bowl. The dog had no manners when it came to drinking and eating. She was well behaved other-wise, so Macy had no real complaints.

Once the noodles were ready, she put her meal to-gether but skipped the garlic bread since her favorite jeans were a little tight. She should probably up her visits to the pool. She hated dieting and her knee still bothered her, so running was out.

Taking a bite of spaghetti, she closed her eyes and moaned about the delicious flavors. The sauce recipe had come from a chef she'd met when she was in Italy, covering the launch of a new political party.

Her cell vibrated on the counter.

Thinking it was Blake, she answered it.

"It's about time," Garrison, her ex, said. The man's voice was as smooth as silk. But the instant she heard it, she cringed.

"Don't hang up. I can hear you breathing. Look, something's coming down the pike and I wanted to give you a—"

"I'll make it simple for you. No. Whatever it is, whatever you think you need to tell me, my answer is no. Don't ever call me again."

She pushed the off button.

The nerve of the man.

Her phone buzzed again. She thought about ignoring it, but she knew he'd just keep calling.

"If I have to change my number to avoid you phoning me I will. I have no interest in anything you have to say. So take whatever is coming down the pike and toss it somewhere, away from me."

There was a long pause. Finally, she'd gotten through to him.

"Um, your receptionist gave me this number to call," Blake's whiskey-coated voice said.

Ahhh!

"Blake, I'm so, so sorry. I— The call before you— Uh, never mind. Yes, of course I wanted you to call."

"Are you okay?" he asked.

"What do you mean?"

"The call. Is someone harassing you?" His voice was measured, but she heard that protective side of him.

"Yes, but it isn't anything I can't handle. It's my former boyfriend. I really am sorry about that. I should have checked my caller ID."

"Do you still want me to look at your books?"

"Yes, but I'm at home. Do you mind coming here, or I can bring them to your house. I've got the ledgers. Everything else is on my laptop. My uncle kept two sets."

"Let me get something to eat, and I'll be over."

"I made spaghetti," she said quickly. "It's my special sauce. That is if you like spaghetti, if you don't—"

"That sounds great. But I have to warn you, I'm

pretty tired. I may not be able to go over everything tonight."

He'd worked hard all day at the feed store and he was still recovering from his injuries. What was she thinking? "I'm being selfish, Blake. You're so strong that sometimes I forget—"

"I'm fine." The steel in his voice made her smile. Never, ever talk about a marine's stamina. She should have known better.

Before she stuck her foot in any deeper, she opted for telling him, "I'll have your food ready when you get here."

"I'm about five minutes out. See you then."

Five minutes? She glanced at herself in the window. Sloppy sweats, mussed hair, her reading glasses on top of her head.

As she ran for the bedroom she gathered her hair into a messy knot on top of her head.

The washer dinged. All of her jeans were wet. She had a choice, flannel pajama bottoms with Dalmatians on them, or the sweats. She went for the dog pants. Then she tried to find a top that kind of matched. She found a black cotton cami that was a little tight, but it would do.

Harley watched her go back and forth as if she were playing both sides in a tennis match.

"I know. But there's no reason I can't look half-decent. It's not like I threw on a sexy cocktail dress."

She wiped the day's mascara off the under part of her eyes and swiped gloss across her lips.

Harley woofed. The truck could be heard pulling into the long drive.

Spritzing perfume, she dashed through it so he wouldn't know she'd only just put it on.

Running to the kitchen she filled a large bowl with noodles and sauce, and set it next to hers. When he rang the bell, she inhaled a deep breath and released it.

Before she reached the door to let Blake in, Harley was there with the handle in her mouth. The door opened about two inches.

"Macy," Blake called.

She cackled. "Harley opened the door, come on in."

He praised the dog every which way and followed Macy to the kitchen.

"Don't you dare tell her how smart she is," she said, laughing. "You could have been a serial killer. I'm going to get a bolt installed higher up, I guess. Or one of those locks that slide down from the top."

He chuckled. "I'm pretty sure she knows how smart she is."

She and Blake ate and chatted about his mom going to take care of his grandmother, and how the store was busier than ever this time of year because it carried hardware, seeds and gardening equipment, holiday decorating items, as well as the stuff for livestock and pets.

"Mom had this great idea to start a pumpkin patch in one of the outer buildings near the store. Normally the pumpkins would be outside, but with all the rain, she was worried about mold. I'll be happy when Halloween is over this weekend so we can get that building clean. We have to check every pumpkin every day to make sure they're okay."

They cleared the dishes, which she put in the dishwasher while he found containers and put the food in the refrigerator. He was a man used to working in a kitchen, and she liked that about him.

"If you're sure you aren't too tired, I've got the laptop set up in the family room. There's a table in there that I use as a desk so I can monitor you-know-who's television viewing habits."

"Now that I've eaten, I feel more awake," he said. "Let me take a look."

She sat on the couch while he sat at the table and wrote things down as he went through the computer files. Every few minutes she'd steal a glance at his profile. But she had to stop before her body overheated. The man made her feel crazy good.

Would it be such a bad thing to scratch the itch? He hadn't said he'd do the story, nevertheless she'd promised him no one else would get the assignment. That took the ethical problem out of the equation.

She had no desire for anything long-term. So far as they were discreet and no one in town would know. They could use his accounting for the paper as a cover. Friends with benefits. She'd never had one of those before.

"Why are you looking at me like that?"

She blinked and realized he was staring at her.

"Uh. You're very handsome."

That sly grin spread across his face. "Huh. Okay."

He turned back to the computer, but continued to grin.

He knew.

"You do bad, bad things to me, Mr. Marine."

The grin grew bigger.

"I haven't touched you," he said, still facing the screen.

"Oh, but you don't even have to," she whispered. Maybe she had one too many glasses of wine with dinner. The room seemed very warm.

That made him look at her.

"Ms. Reynolds, are you coming on to me?"

"Yes, sir. I believe I am. What are you going to do about it?"

He sat there for a few seconds, his dark brown eyes catching her gaze as if he were searching for answers.

"What about your ethical dilemma?"

"I'm not writing the story, so it's no longer a problem. I wouldn't be dating the subject of one of my stories. You'd just be another guy."

"So if I ask you on a date, you'd say yes?"

She nodded. "With a few conditions."

He leaned an elbow on the table, but didn't take his eyes off her. "I'm not surprised."

"They're nothing wild. First, we keep it simple. You mentioned that you need simple right now and so do I. So we set some ground rules, and everyone is happy."

"And those would be?"

"We are discreet and exclusive."

He frowned. "Why discreet? Are you ashamed to be seen with me?"

"Don't be silly. You're the hottest man I've ever seen. *Ever.* I'd be more than happy to show you off to anyone who would look. But I'm new to the town, and— I don't know. I just think it would be best. That is, since we are keeping it simple."

Now that she'd said it out loud, it seemed over the top.

"Listen, normally, I'd have no problem. But one of the benefits of our mutual companionship, other than the obvious, is that it would detract a lot of the ladies from pushing their single daughters at me. My brother saw a picture of me on a social media site today loading feed bags into a customer's truck. I didn't even know someone was taking pictures. And why would anyone care?"

She smiled. "Remind me to find out what site that is. I want a copy. I heard you had your shirt off."

He huffed. "This is what I'm talking about. How about we hold hands in public or something. Let me take you on a few dates. People date all the time. It doesn't have to mean forever."

"Okay. I see your point. And since I want this to be exclusive, for however long it lasts, it would make sense for others to know. And in this town, it's probably impossible to be discreet."

"Yep. So we're friends who date. Is there anything else?"

"Well, I was kind of hoping that there would be benefits besides dating."

He frowned. "Like what?"

She chewed on her lip. Did he really need her to spell it out for him? "When the time comes, if you're into it, maybe we could—you know."

He grinned and cocked the right side of his mouth. "I'd definitely be into that."

"Me, too." *In fact, we can start right now.*

"So will you go out with me on Halloween? A friend of mine is throwing a party."

She bit her lip. A movie or dinner date was one thing. Meeting his friends was another.

"You're going to say no, aren't you?"

"Uh, well, it depends. It seems a little fast to be meeting the friends. But that isn't the reason I'm hesitant. I promised to help out at the shelter that night. We're dressing up our pets in costumes and handing candy out to kids to raise awareness about the facility."

"Not a problem. I'll help you, and then we'll go to the party afterward."

"Deal. Is it a costume party?"

"Yes, but it doesn't need to be anything fancy."

"Okay. Cherie is sending me a costume to wear for the shelter event. She is really into Halloween and has a ton of stuff in storage. It will probably be a giant pink rabbit or something, so I apologize in advance."

He laughed. "That's some friend."

"You have no idea."

He stood and went over to the couch where he stuck out his hand. When she put hers in his, he pulled her to her feet.

"It's a bit preemptive, but I've wanted to do this since the day I met you."

His mouth was on hers before she blinked. His lips were softer than expected. When his hand cupped her chin, she sighed with pleasure.

"You taste so good," he said against her mouth.

"It's the sauce," she whispered back as he trailed kisses down her neck.

"No, babe, it's you." Then his mouth returned to hers and their kiss intensified, so familiar, so easy, as if they'd done this a million times before.

When he lifted his head, they both gasped for air. "I think I'd better go," he said, leaning his forehead against hers. "I'm not sure I can control myself much longer. I want you so bad it hurts."

She glanced down, reached out and caressed him.

Hissing, he broke away from her. "Macy, please. I—"

"I want you," she said. "Now." She met his gaze and smiled a warm, wide smile.

"But I planned to take you out and woo you," he said. His voice strained.

"Woo me? Do people still say that?" She undid the buckle on his jeans.

"Yes. I say that. Remember, this is Texas. We like to court our women." Even though he didn't have much of an accent he put an extra twang in there.

"I'm a Yankee woman. We don't need wooing. We just need hot, fit marines who make us think of naughty, naughty things to do."

He chuckled. "I'm beginning to like the North better and better every second. Are you sure?"

"Yes," she replied as she tugged his head down to hers.

9

AFTER THEY MADE sure Harley was settled with the largest rawhide bone he'd ever seen, Blake trailed the raven-haired siren to her bedroom. The rest of the house was decorated in rich leather and textured walls. But her room had white walls, white furniture and most of the bedding was the same color. Only the pillows on the bed were pale blue.

He was about to comment on her style, it fit her in a feminine but classic way, when she slipped off her top. A lacy black bra with a tiny red bow in the center cupped her lush breasts.

"You're beautiful."

Her cheeks turned pink. She had no idea how attractive she was.

She pointed to him.

"Your turn."

She was nervous, he could see the slight tension around her eyes and the trembling in her fingers. He was sensitive to her emotions. As if his body and mind had been tuned to her like a radio dial.

He slipped his T-shirt off.

Her mouth formed an O.

"Wow, you're amazing." She didn't hold back.

He liked that about her.

"You're gorgeous, so much so that I can't get you out of my head. You've been keeping me up nights. Once I saw you doing everything you could to heave Harley into the back of your car, I knew I wanted you."

She slipped her baggy pajama bottoms off, and he sucked in a breath. The panties matched the bra. A red ribbon bow on each hip held the tiny triangles of fabric together. Her long legs were those of a runner, strong and firm. Curvy hips, sparkling eyes, and those breasts, she was all woman, and his fantasy come true.

It occurred to him that in seconds she would see the evidence of that, but he didn't want to stop the game.

"Oh" was all she said as he undid his zipper and his hard cock revealed. "It's a— That is, okay, yes. It's really— Yeah. Impressive."

He chuckled.

"Beets!" she said suddenly and put a hand to her temple.

Was she ill?

"Beets?"

"We don't have condoms. At least, I don't." She shook her head. "Tofu turkey!"

"Do you always say food names when you're upset?"

"What? No, it's that I don't like to swear. My

mouth, uh, let's just say hanging out with military types and reporters has left me with a mouth like a—"

"A marine?"

She smiled. "Yelling curse words upset the animals, so I say foods I'm not super fond of to keep from saying the things I shouldn't. Do you have any condoms?"

"Not on me. But I have an idea."

She smirked. "It better not involve driving to a store and buying some. I don't think I can wait that long."

No way he could wait that long, either. Besides, he was worried that she might change her mind. He'd respect her wishes, of course, but he'd also be very disappointed.

"Hold that thought." He rezippered and left the house, heading for the driveway.

Opening the toolbox in the back of his truck he dug around for the first-aid kit. There he found two foil packages. When he'd gone through boot camp it had been drilled into his head that you always packed protection.

He kissed the packets before slamming everything shut and bolting for the door. Praying they hadn't lost the moment, he found Macy curled up in her bed with the covers to her neck.

He tossed the packets to her, and she caught them in the air.

"Quick reflexes," he said as he pulled off his boots and shoved away his jeans. "Is everything okay? You can still say no. You can always say no. I want you to know that."

She rolled her eyes and as a welcoming gesture tossed back his side of the covers. "Blake, I was freezing. That's why I got in here. I want you and I don't want to wait any longer." He slid in. She grinned as she ripped open one of the foil packages and leaned over him.

"Slow down," he said, coughing out a laugh. "You don't have to be in such a hurry."

"But I am." She palmed his erection. And he was about to lose that sense of control he'd warned her about.

"We've got all night." He struggled to get the words out without moaning.

"Yes, but I've been fantasizing about you, about us like this, for days." Before he could stop her, she rolled the condom down over him. When she had finished, he caught her wrist and brought her fingers to his mouth and kissed them.

Damn, that might have been the sexiest thing any woman had ever said to him, which made him all the more determined to make this last. Moving her onto her back, he propped her underneath him.

His right hand slid between them, his fingers seeking her heat.

She smiled and arched her back, clearly wanting and welcoming him.

"I want to do this. For you, Macy," he said, speaking softly into her ear. Her body arched again. "Knowing every inch of you is important to me." He rose up and sat back. It wasn't the most comfortable position for him, but he didn't care about the pain. "Put your legs over my shoulders, baby."

She started to say something, but she stopped. Taking one of the larger pillows, he tucked it under her. He intended to give her every pleasure he possibly could and this would make that easier.

"I—"

"What?" he asked, as he touched her breasts, teasing her.

"I haven't really..." she said, leaving the thought unfinished.

"That sounds like a challenge, Macy."

"No, it's—"

She drew in a sharp breath as his mouth stoked her rising passion. Encouraged by her growing cries and murmurs, he was intent on satisfying every inch of her.

When she called out his name, her body quaked in its release and she reached out for him. He gathered her in his arms and held her tight.

"I need you, Blake." Her body had almost stopped thrumming. "Now."

"Bossy, aren't you?" He dropped a quick kiss on her lips. Tossing the pillow aside, he rolled on to his back. With his leg the way it was, it would be easier if she was on top. His thigh was throbbing, but so were other parts of him.

A limp noodle, he drew her to him. Her soft thick hair had fallen from its messy knot creating a dark veil around her silver-green eyes and high cheekbones. She was so sexy.

His hard cock poked playfully at her belly. She smiled at him. "Finally." Lifting up, she positioned herself on him and sighed as she rocked back and forth.

He matched her pace. It wasn't easy with his beautiful nymph riding him with wild abandon. She increased their tempo and he groaned out his approval.

As her muscles contracted, he held on—barely—and told her to open her eyes.

The moonlight streaming through her window bathed her face in a gorgeous way, and her eyes met his.

"You're incredible," he told her.

She moved faster, pressing into him, never slowing until they'd lost their grip and climaxed together. Losing control had never felt so good.

"That was better than any dream," she whispered tiredly as she fell onto his chest.

He cradled her and murmured sweet words that made her sigh. In minutes, she was fast asleep.

A whine from the doorway had him sliding out from under his beautiful fairy, and pulling the comforter up to keep her warm.

She grumbled but her head stayed on the pillow.

He slipped on his jeans and T-shirt and let Harley out via the back door. He watched her as she ran around the yard a few times. The moon reflected off the lake, and he envied Macy this view.

At the thought of her name, something tugged in his gut, a warning that he might be headed for trouble.

Making love to her was definitely not going to scratch his itch. It only made him want her all the more.

Slow. He reminded himself. She'd just run from a

bad relationship, and he was in no shape to start anything serious. It wouldn't be fair to either of them.

Harley bounded inside and gulped some water. She then grabbed a chew toy and made for her bed. Lying next to the toy, she went to sleep.

What a dog.

He'd never seen anything like her, and he just loved her.

Her owner was equally unusual in a way that called to him.

Shutting off the lights, he considered his next move. He should go home, but it didn't seem right to leave Macy without saying goodbye.

Digging in his pocket, he found one of his pills. After breaking it in half, he drank it down with a glass of water. He slid back into bed with Macy.

"Thanks for letting her out," she said as she snuggled against his chest. He tightened his arms around her, bringing her close.

"No problem. Go to sleep, angel."

"You wore me out," she said quietly. "I don't have a choice."

That made him smile.

"You didn't have to stay, but I'm really glad you did." Her words were soft and heartfelt.

"I may be gone by the time you wake up for work. But trust me, I'd like to stay for the next couple of days. Right here in this bed with you."

"Mmm. I like having friends like you."

Friends? In the plural?

As far as he was concerned, he would be her only

friend like this for a very long time. The thought of another man's hands on her— Hell.

He'd already become one of those possessive blockheads.

She didn't deserve that.

He looked down at her sweet face.

But dammit. She was his.

10

WHEN MACY OPENED her front door to him two days later, Blake's jaw dropped open. He looked at her from head to toe, his eyes resting a bit longer on her midsection and breasts.

She scoffed and turned away. "I'm going to kill Cherie the next time I see her," she grumbled. "I can't wear this. It's—it's…inappropriate."

"Sexy as hell," Blake said at the same time.

"Maybe if it was only you and me, but I'm not wearing this genie costume to pass out candy to little kids."

Closing the door behind him, he followed her into the house. "It's not as revealing as you think," he said. "All of you is covered. It's that some of the material is flesh-colored. And you're not pretending to be from the Arabian Nights or something—that's a kids' story. Besides there are ballerinas, princesses and fairies running around all over the place."

She rolled her eyes. "It's not really a kids' story! A king kills a thousand virgins after he defiles them.

Most of the kids are under seven. And it's too late. I don't have anything else to wear."

"It's cold out, and the temperature might drop down to the thirties. Maybe you could just wear a sweater or something. The skirt isn't that bad with all the scarves." He eyed her appreciatively. "Do those scarves come off one by one?"

The man really did have a one-track mind.

She growled at him.

"That's good," he chuckled. "We can just paint your face to look like a tiger. By the way—hello. I missed you a lot today."

He snagged her and wrapped his arms around her. Instantly, she forgot her troubles as his tongue tangled with hers. Pressing herself into him, his hard cock poked back.

That she could do that to him pleased her. More than she wanted to admit. Every time he looked at her, she felt like the most beautiful woman in the world.

She'd smiled so much today that Amanda asked her if she was okay. When Macy gave her the afternoon off to get her brothers ready to trick-or-treat, the shock and gratitude on the young woman's face had been truly remarkable.

"As much as I want to stay here, I have to get to the animal shelter. I'm the only one who has a key to the locker where all the candy is stored. Mariel, the office manager, didn't trust herself with it. So I had to hide all the candy in my locker."

"We better get going. Where's the beast?"

"Outside. Chasing the geese dumb enough to land within her radius. She's been after them for at least an hour. I'm not worried about her catching one. Every time she gets close to them they honk at her, and she runs away. It's one of her games she's made up. I'll get her."

When she returned, he had Harley's leash and a few toys for the dog to play with while they handed out candy.

Blake had spent the past few nights here, rising early in the morning to be at the feed store. But their lovemaking in the evenings was epic. No man had ever taken her to such heights. She was kind of angry that she'd been missing out on so much.

In his arms, Macy knew it was the safest she'd ever felt. Even though it was only a temporary harbor, she enjoyed it. And he slept when he was with her. Plagued my insomnia and night terrors, he'd had neither since they'd been together.

He'd admitted as much the night before last. She'd laughed it off and said it was because she wore him out. But the look in his eyes, that deep, searching gaze of his, told her it was much more than that. She'd become his port in a storm, as well.

Scary how intimate and intense a relationship could become when both parties were in need of the same thing. They read each other on a more profound level. And he was kind and generous to a fault.

In a mere few days, her cold, jaded heart had realized it had been missing out on what a real relationship could be.

Except, that this was just a fling.

I must keep telling myself that.

Harley, who sat in the back of Blake's truck, on her

special blanket, licked Macy's elbow. It was almost as if she wanted to tell her, *you'll be okay. You have me.*

Reaching behind, she scratched the dog's ear.

And for that I'm grateful.

It didn't take them long to arrive at the animal shelter, but still, bunches of children dressed in an array of costumes had already climbed the hill and gotten there ahead of them.

Blake had assisted with the carving of several pumpkins, which adorned the front porch and the lobby. For safety's sake they had put battery-operated candles inside the jack-o'-lanterns. A good idea, since the first thing Harley did was step in one on the way into the building.

She freaked out until Blake was able to get her paw out of the offending orange ball. Harley growled at it.

"Bad jack-o'-lantern, bad." Blake wagged a finger at the pumpkin, which seemed to please the dog.

Blake put Harley's dragon ears and scales on her. They'd been another gift from Cherie. The scales covered the dog's back and buckled around her belly and neck. The ears were on a headband of sorts.

She pranced around as if she were the queen of everything.

"You are the cutest dragon I've ever seen," Blake muttered as he scratched her behind the ears.

Back outside, Macy kept her coat on. She got a kick out of watching Blake interact with all the kids. He'd worn jeans and a T-shirt that had the *Avengers* logo on it. He'd told her he wasn't much into costumes.

By eight, the crowds had thinned out. That was fine since they were almost out of candy.

"That went by a lot faster than I expected," he said.

"You were great. The kids loved you, and you definitely know your superheroes."

He laughed. "I love to read, and comic books were cheap when I was a kid. I had a habit of losing library books, so my mom only let me take one out a week. Comic books were a cheap alternative."

The man was nothing but contradictions. He was definitely more than a pretty face. He was as tough as they came, but he was also intelligent and thoughtful.

Everything a woman could want, and then some.

And he wanted her.

"What's going on?" he asked as he shifted into Drive and steered the truck away from the shelter.

"Hmm? Oh. Honestly, I'm sort of awed by how amazing you are. What I don't understand is why me? When you could quite obviously have a fling with any woman you wanted."

At the stop sign, he glanced over at her. "That you don't see how beautiful, smart and funny you are is one of the reasons I like you so much. Why would I want anyone else when I have you?"

If Harley's enormous head wasn't on the armrest between them, Macy might have moved into his lap right then and there. "You really do always know what to say."

The street he turned onto was crowded with cars on both sides. She loved this part of Tranquil Waters. Many of the houses had been built in the early 1900s. The neighborhood was decked out in fall colors and

Halloween decorations. People were out in their yards chatting while kids ran around in their costumes.

"It's going to be a hike to find somewhere to park. Do you want me to drop you off in front of my friend's place?"

Definitely not. The last thing she wanted to do was walk into a party where she knew no one—in a skimpy genie costume. "I'm up for a walk. I had my fair share of candy tonight. Are you sure it's okay to bring Harley?"

"Yep. Jaime loves dogs."

She'd never brought a dog the size of a horse to a party.

"No! I can't believe I forgot."

"What?"

"A gift. Your rule about always bringing a gift to a party. I've been rushing around and I didn't remember to get anything."

He grinned. "Don't worry. I've got us covered. I had flowers delivered earlier today from the both of us. One of those fall bouquets. Jaime loves flowers."

Wait. Jaime was a girl? He'd been telling her stories the past couple of days about how he and Jaime were always in trouble together as kids.

Before she could mention it, they were at the door of one of the largest homes on the block. A wrap-around porch and two-story columns gave it a plantation house feel.

The open door led into a foyer the shape and size of a rotunda. It was a fit for the Southern mansion. Dark wood floors graced the area, and a huge round table with a bouquet of flowers sat below a crystal chandelier. There were two staircases with banisters draped in magnolia garlands.

"Oh. My. God! It's my favorite marine." A woman in a formfitting Catwoman suit threw her arms around Blake and kissed him hard on the mouth.

And he didn't seem to mind a bit.

"Hey, stinky. What's up?"

"You're late," she said when she stepped back and eyed him up and down. "And you aren't wearing a costume. I told you that you had to wear a costume."

"You know I don't do costumes. I was giving a hand out at the animal shelter, which is why I'm late." That seemed to remind him that she was standing there. "This is my friend Macy," he said as he put an arm around her shoulders.

The happy smile faded from the woman's face as she gave Macy the once-over.

"You that Yankee newspaper editor?"

"Jaime, be nice," Blake warned, but with a playful tone to his voice.

Refusing to back down, Macy jutted out her chin. "Yes."

"This is who you're dating? Do we not have enough women in the South that you have to start in on the Northerners?"

Blake pointed a finger at his friend. "I *really* like her, so play nice. I mean it."

Her hero. Macy smiled up at him.

"What, for goodness' sake, is that?"

Harley cocked her head.

"That's Macy's dog, Harley," he answered.

Jaime glanced back at Macy. "Great Dane?"

"Yes."

The woman smiled at her. Then she put two fingers to her mouth and blew an earsplitting whistle.

A dark gray, almost blue, Great Dane with silvery eyes trotted into the room.

"Harley, this is Bruno."

"If you don't want that costume shredded in the next five minutes, I suggest you take if off of Harley. Bruno gets jealous when other dogs have things he doesn't. Though, I'm definitely going to get him a costume for next year because that dragon outfit is too cute."

Macy wondered if the dog might attack Harley, and she put herself between the two animals.

"Oh, don't worry. He wouldn't hurt a fly. But he would try to get that outfit off of her for himself. He loves everything with ruffles, patterns and either brown or green."

Blake took the costume off of Harley and she shook herself.

"Now, Bruno, play nice. Take her out to the clubhouse."

The dog glanced back at his owner and nodded.

Were all Great Danes so smart?

"Are you sure they'll be okay?" Macy wasn't worried about Bruno being with Harley, she was concerned as to how Harley would interact with him. She got along with the other dogs at the shelter, but she'd always been supervised.

"I'm sure," Jaime said. "Blake, go say hello to everyone. I want to speak to your Yankee lady."

Blake stared at Macy. "I think that might make her uncomfortable. It's probably best if I stick around."

Macy appreciated that he wanted to stay by her, but she wasn't a child.

"Don't worry, I won't bite her," Jaime promised. "Besides, anyone with a dog like that is okay in my book. Great Danes are sensitive and bright, and extremely needy. They take a lot of love, time and patience. That's something your Yankee will need if she's going to train you up, as well."

Blake rolled his eyes.

Macy laughed.

Jaime made a shooing motion with her hands. "Go on. She'll join you in a minute."

"I'm okay," she assured him. "I'll find you when we're done."

Curious about why Jaime wanted her alone, she encouraged him to go.

Jaime reached out to shake her hand. "Sorry about that. I'm a bit protective of him," she said. "He's like a brother to me."

Weird, she'd never seen anyone kiss a brother like that, but Macy kept her mouth shut. She shook the woman's hand.

"You have a great house," Macy said. Her mind was awhirl with questions.

"Belonged to my great-grandma. We've tried to keep the restoration accurate, but it isn't easy."

She motioned for Macy to follow her.

"We'll put your coat in here." Jamie stood in front of a long hall closet and held out her hand for the garment.

"I—that is, my costume's quite revealing."

The woman judged her warily. "It can't be any more revealing than mine, or some of the others in here. Tara has a French maid's outfit on. Every time she bends over to get some food, she flashes her red thong to the entire room. It can't be any worse than that."

Macy slipped off the coat, feeling exposed.

"Well, you are as pretty as he said. It's not fair that you have those legs and that chest."

She wasn't sure how to respond to that...compliment?

"He's head over heels for you."

"What?" The sudden change in topic had Macy's mind spinning.

"Blake. We've never seen him like this over a woman. He called every single person at this party and told them they'd better welcome you or else." She laughed at Macy's grimace. "I know. But he's protective that way. I like the fact that you stood up to me back there. I have a feeling you and I could be friends. But there's just one thing you should know."

"What's that?" Macy walked next to her as they entered the living room full of people.

"If you hurt him, I will do the same to you." The threat was undeniable. "And I always mean exactly what I say."

Macy was about to tell the woman to back off, but she was equally protective of Blake. "If it makes you feel any better, I think he's the most incredible man I've ever met."

Jaime seemed to be in shock. "Oh, you have it just

as bad for him. Interesting. I can't wait to see how this plays out."

She wasn't sure about what to make of that comment, but across the room she spotted someone she knew.

"Excuse me, I see a friend of mine."

Josh, the veterinarian from the shelter, stood by a bay window talking to another guest.

When he saw her, he smiled brightly. "Hey," he said and hugged her, "I didn't know you'd be here." He left an arm around her shoulders, which she didn't mind at the moment. She was grateful to have at least one other person, besides Blake, be nice to her.

She shrugged. "I'm on a date. He was the one who was invited."

Josh's eyes widened in surprise. "Good, good. Seems like you're assimilating into the town really well. Let me introduce you to Brendan Tucker. He and his wife, Jaime, are the hosts of the party."

Macy shook the man's hand.

"I met your wife," she said, searching for something polite to say.

The two men laughed. "She can be a bit much, but she's a sweetheart once you get to know her," Brendan said.

"I'll have to take your word on that. Frankly, I've dealt with insurgents who were less scary."

The men howled.

"So who's your date?" Josh asked.

"I am," a deep voice said from behind them. "And I'd appreciate it if you'd get your hands off my woman."

"Blake," Macy admonished. It made little sense. Why would he act so jealous? It was ridiculous. They barely knew each other and Josh was a genuine good guy.

"Who's going to make me?" Josh said with heat in his voice.

What was happening here?

Macy ducked away from Josh's arm and stood apart from the two men. They were glaring at each another.

"I am, jerk." Blake stepped forward.

"Now, fellas. You know Jaime will have a fit if you break anything. Everyone calm down," Brendan cajoled.

"Why did you have your arm around Macy?" Blake growled at Josh.

"She's my friend. We went out a couple of times when she first came to town. What's the big deal? You aren't still mad at me after all this time? I wasn't the one who made you write those letters."

"Wait a minute," Blake whispered harshly. "You two dated."

His snapped around to look at Macy as if she were some kind of traitor.

She'd had enough.

"I don't know what's wrong with the two of you, but you're embarrassing me."

"Answer the question, Macy. Did you date my former best friend?"

His former best friend?

Oh. Ohhhh. This must be some male feud and

she'd stepped right into the middle of it. "Two times," she replied.

"And that was it," Josh said. "We knew from the get-go that we weren't right for each other. But we are friends. She volunteers at the shelter so we see each other occasionally."

Blake's mouth formed a thin line. He focused in on Macy. "You never mentioned that you went out with anyone in town."

"You never asked. And anyway, nothing happened with your former best friend. You're acting so foolish. Both of you."

With that she stomped out in search of her dog. She would not put up with that kind of arrogant behavior from any man. She and Blake were causal. He had no right to—

She froze in midstep. Hadn't she felt the same about him when his friend Jaime had kissed him?

I was as jealous, just not as vocal about it.

"Hey, genie, why don't you come over here and grant me my three wishes?" a man in a Frankenstein costume called out. A crowd stood around him.

They all laughed.

She turned her back on them.

"Told you the Yankee girl was a witch."

These people were beyond rude.

"You know what, Frankenstein, so much for that Southern hospitality you folks talk about. I'm proud to be from the North. In fact—"

"George, are you giving Macy a hard time? Because if you are, I'm going to have some serious words with you," Jaime said as slipped her arm through Macy's in a clear sign of solidarity. "This is Blake's girl, so that means she's like family. And you know how I feel about my family. You all apologize right now."

Without hesitation, apologies were quickly issued.

"Forgive me, Macy," George said. "I'd blame the whiskey, but sometimes I'm simply an old fool. Just ask my three ex-wives."

The crowd chuckled, the tension evaporated instantly.

Macy looked to Jaime so they wouldn't see her smile. "You didn't have to do that," she told her.

"I meant what I said. I'm sorry about before. This couldn't have been fun for you what with friends fighting, George being his stupid self and me acting like, well, we know what I was acting like."

Macy shrugged. "I've been to worse parties."

Jaime guffawed. "You're all right. I need to check on the caterers in the kitchen. Come with me?"

What she really wanted was to go home, but she followed Jaime.

The kitchen bustled with servers and food preparers sprinting around and shouting.

"Pietro, those mushroom caps are a hit."

One of the guys in a chef's hat blew Jaime a kiss before opening one of the ovens to put in a tray of what looked like hors d'oeuvres.

Walking along the kitchen island, big enough for a dozen bar stools, Jaime inspected the food. Then she grabbed a plate and took food from several of the trays. She handed the plate to Macy. "This one's for you."

She loaded up another plate. "This one's for me. I

never get to eat when I throw parties, but I'm starved. Come on, let's go check on the dogs."

"Are Blake and Josh all right, do you think?"

Jaime laughed. "My husband is there, and they're scared to death of him. They won't get too out of hand."

"Why are they scared of him?"

"Because he's the only man who can tame me, so he must be one real son of a gun. And he is. I talk tough, but I'd do anything for that man. The love of my life, and he knows it."

Next door to the kitchen was the breakfast room, which looked out over a pool area. Macy could see Harley chasing Bruno around the cabana. The two dogs stopped for a second, and then Bruno began chasing Harley.

"They're pals already, see?" Jaime sat on one of the loungers and leaned back a heated lamp nearby. She put the plate of food on her chest and started eating.

Macy sat on a lounger next to her.

"Sorry," Jaime said after swallowing a bite-size quiche. "I haven't had anything but water and vegetables for a week so I'd fit in this damn costume."

Macy grinned. "Hey, it worked. You look incredible."

"Thanks for that. And I really am sorry about earlier. When we heard Blake was injured this time, well, we're all kind of protective of him. He's always been such a stand-up type of guy. And I didn't lie, he is like my brother. He has dated in the past, obviously, but—I've never seen him like he is with you. I noticed him when Josh hugged you. He'd been giving you the loving eyes from across the room, and then it was like a cartoon. I was surprised steam didn't come out of his ears when Josh put his arm around your shoulders.

"And shame on Josh for egging Blake on. That's one of those man things, pushing each other's buttons, I guess."

Macy should have seen this coming. It hadn't been that long since she'd been away from Garrison, although it sure seemed like it.

"I went on a couple of friendly dates with Josh, nothing happened," Macy offered. "But for some reason Blake seems to think I should have been a nun before I met him. Bunch of macho nonsense, if you ask me." Macy bit into something with bacon and cheese in the shape of a ball. It was heaven.

"Yes, it is. Things seem to be moving fast between you two."

Macy winced. "I'm not sure what I'm supposed to say. We both agreed that this would be a casual arrangement."

"Blake's way past casual," Jaime said.

"It's only been a couple of days. I mean, I've known him maybe two weeks. Don't get me wrong— I like him a lot." More than she would admit to one of his best friends. "I'm not sure what to do. Maybe I should slow it down until we both get our bearings."

"Good luck with that." Jaime pointed toward the house.

"There you are," Blake said worriedly.

"See ya, kiddies. I need to get back to my party. Blake, behave yourself. Macy, it was so nice to meet you. I mean that. I'm going to stop by the paper soon and take you to lunch."

"I'd like that," Macy said.

Blake took Jaime's place on the lounger, but he sat sideways facing Macy. They sat in silence for a full thirty seconds.

"I'd like to blame it on the pain pills or too much alcohol, but the truth is I haven't had any because I knew I'd be driving," he said quickly.

Macy stared down at her plate, no longer hungry.

"There's no excuse for that kind of behavior. I just saw his arm around you, and— I promise you it will never happen again."

"You embarrassed me."

"I embarrassed both of us. And I'm truly sorry, Macy."

She still didn't meet his eyes, but she noticed he wrung his hands.

Give the guy a break.

She lifted her head. "I should be flattered about the show you put on in there, but I'm not. I don't like bullies and I'm certainly not someone's possession. I don't belong to you, Blake. I'm an individual. I've been on my own for a long, long time."

He sighed. "You're right. It's a mess. Do you want me to have somebody drive you home? Or I'm happy to do it, if it's okay with you. I just don't want you to be afraid of me."

Macy shook her head. "I'm not afraid of you. I could never be afraid of you. You wouldn't hurt me, no matter what the circumstances. But it does bother me that you think I would be scared of you. You're one of the kindest men I've ever met. And so gentle with Harley…and me. And I don't think any of those guests would appreciate having a hundred-and-seventy-five-pound dog in their backseat, so yes, I'm okay with you taking us home."

"We're okay, then?"

"We are but you have to remember I'm not your favorite toy that you get upset when someone else touches it." She frowned. "That didn't come out right."

"You kind of are," he said under his breath.

"What?"

"Not a toy, but you are my favorite person. Ever."

She couldn't hide her smile. "Stop with the Mr. Charming routine. I'm supposed to be mad at you."

He smiled back.

They said their goodbyes, found Harley and climbed into his truck.

"I was beginning to worry, though. You did seem a bit too perfect," she finally said when they exited off the highway and turned onto her street.

"I'm a lot of things, Macy, but I'm far from perfect."

A few minutes later they were in her driveway.

"Thanks for the ride," she said. As he went to switch off the truck, she stopped him. "I'm really tired. I think Harley and I will say good-night here."

That emotionless mask slipped over his face, he nodded. "I understand."

"No," she said, as she opened the door for Harley, "I don't think you do. It's as much my fault as it is yours that this thing between us has been moving at the speed of light. You were the one who suggested wooing. I haven't forgotten that. A little space would be good so we can both think about what it is we want."

"You," he said. "I just want you."

She stepped up and leaned into the truck to kiss him lightly on the lips. "I want you, too. But with our recent histories, it's not such a bad idea to take a break."

He gave her a brief nod.

Harley ran over to the gate Macy used regularly to get into the house. It was the closest entrance to the driveway. The truck didn't move until she'd gone in and put on the lights.

He slowly backed out of the driveway and she sighed when the headlights hit the road.

Picking up her phone, she dialed Cherie.

"I'm the biggest idiot in the world," she said.

"Tell me something I don't know," her friend replied.

11

"I'M AN IDIOT." Blake stomped upstairs to his bedroom. "Certifiable." Stripping, he turned on the shower as hot as he could stand it. He'd gone and lost the best thing that had ever happened to him.

As much as he wanted to blame Josh, it was his fault for acting like a jealous goof. For the life of him, he didn't understand why he'd lost his cool.

That wasn't true.

He stuck his head under the water.

The woman tied him in knots; she was unlike anyone he'd ever met before. And he didn't know what to do with himself.

Hell, he couldn't even remember what he'd said to Josh. And for a few seconds, when he found out they'd been on a date, he'd been furious. The image of his friend possibly kissing her—or worse—had made him livid.

Because she was his.

He slammed a fist against the tile.

Get a grip, man.

You break something in your mother's house there really will be something to answer for. Leaning both arms forward, he let the hot water run down his back.

She'd just gotten out of a relationship with an idiot, and here he was acting like one. He didn't treat women that way, and if his mother ever found out she'd be so disappointed.

That was the answer. He had to talk to his mom. She'd know how he could persuade his favorite journalist to give him another chance. It meant confessing what he'd done, and she wouldn't be happy. But she'd give him good advice; she was always wise when it came to relationships. Until the day his dad died, his parents had had one of the best marriages he'd ever seen.

He wanted that with Macy. It was too fast, and his head knew it. But his heart told him she was the one.

Now he had to convince her of that.

After finishing the shower and checking close to make sure he hadn't broken one of the tiles, Blake picked up the phone.

"What were you thinking?" his mother bellowed, she didn't even bother to say hello. "I did not raise you to act that way!"

Someone, probably Jaime, must have already called her to say what a moron he'd been at the party.

"Yes, ma'am. I don't have an excuse."

"I agree, young man. If I were there I'd box your ears. That poor girl, in a house full of people she didn't know, and then you went all King Kong on her."

"Shame on you," he heard his grandmother say.

Why did I call? He glanced at the heavens.

"You aren't telling me anything I don't already know. I feel like the world's biggest jerk. And I swear it will never happen again."

"What have I told you about swearing?"

"Yes, ma'am. Please, tell me how to fix this."

"*That's* the most sensible thing you've said all night."

"Halleluiah!" shouted a chorus of women.

"Mom, am I on speaker? And who else is there?"

"Yes, and just a few ladies from Momma's quilting circle."

Blake palmed his face.

"You listen to what we have to say, boy," Momma D shouted. She didn't seem too sick to him. "We'll explain to you how to set things right with that Yankee, and you don't mess it up again. You hear me?"

"Yes, ma'am."

"Now get a pencil, this is going to be a long list," his mother ordered.

And a very long night.

THREE DAYS HAD gone by, and except for two texts, she hadn't heard from Blake or even seen him and it wasn't for a lack of trying. Twice she'd gone to the feed store to pick up food for Harley, and then later some nails that she didn't need, but he wasn't there.

The first text had been an apology. She'd already forgiven him so it wasn't necessary. At the end he had asked about the types of questions he could ask the servicemen and -women for the story. He'd said that he'd meant to tell her the night he worked on her books, that he wanted to do the articles, but he'd been distracted by other things.

By her throwing herself at him, she was certain.

She sent him a text back explaining that he didn't have to apologize, and she was looking forward to seeing him soon. She also emailed him a bunch of questions for the interviews and offered to help him in any way necessary.

He'd replied with, "Thank you."

That was it.

She reread her email again to make sure she hadn't said anything he could misconstrue, but she hadn't.

Stupid marine. She missed him. As much as she didn't want to admit it to herself, she had become quite attached to him.

More than likely she'd wounded his pride. What if he decided she was too much trouble and had moved on? She thought about the women at the café who were so enamored with the half-naked marine. He was bright, gentlemanly and as hot as they came.

And she'd been upset because why? Oh, yeah, because he'd cared for her so much that he went all crazy macho for her.

Cherie was right. She was a class A idiot.

"Some guy beats his chest for you, and you have to be all I'm Miss Independence and don't you dare like me too much," Cherie had chastised.

"But men should not be allowed to—"

"What? Be men. He was staking his territory. It's classic male behavior. Could he have handled it better? Yes. But they don't call them male rivalries for nothing, doll. There's history there. Probably a lot of crap you know nothing about. He apologized profusely and you came back with you needed a break. How else is he supposed to interpret that?"

"But he got so weird when he found out Josh and I dated a couple of times. It was strange."

"Macy," Cherie scolded, "you are not this dense. Oh, wait, you were attached to that boss of yours."

"Geez. All right. I get it. But explain to me how I can feel so much for him so fast. I thought I was in love with Garrison, but it doesn't come close to what I feel for Blake. It scares me. And it's hot and wonderful now, well, it was. But doesn't that kind of thing burn out fast. Isn't it better to slow it down before we both get hurt?"

Cherie barked out a loud laugh. "Honey, when you feel what you do, there's no meaningful reason to slow things down. You said it yourself, you're afraid. And you've been hurt, so your defenses are up. That's actually a good thing. But from everything you've told me, this guy's the real deal. If you get your heart broken, at least it was by a guy who deserved you. Oh, and the sex is great. Do you have any idea how difficult it is to find a guy like your marine?

"I haven't found a single one and I've been looking. Trust me. You need to be a grown-up and reach out to him."

Pursing her lips, she tried to forget the rest of her conversation with Cherie and focus on the story in front of her. It was deadline day and she didn't have any more time to waste. An hour later, she'd edited two pieces and had all but the ad pages ready to go.

The quality of talent in a town as small as Tranquil Waters had genuinely surprised her. It was full of artists and writers. Many of whom liked the idea of more reporting about the community writ large. She'd even found a good photographer to cover local sports.

High school football was a religion to many in this region and state. She'd discovered that if she had sports photos on the front page, then circulation went up. In turn, she'd hired a couple of freelancers to do personal stories on the most popular players and their families and neighbors. Next on her to-do list was to tap into other important local hobbies and interests.

Now when she went into the café, people actually smiled and waved at her. All it took was a little effort.

Everything at work seemed to be falling into place. Meanwhile, her heart was breaking.

This wasn't the first time and it probably wouldn't be the last that the aspects of her life would not be in harmony all at once.

Blake's friend Jaime had even called to find out whether she was okay. That was how Macy found out he was in a foul mood and that no one wanted to be around him. She'd advised Macy to sit tight and wait for him to realize what he'd done wrong, which was the exact opposite of what Cherie had said.

Amanda knocked on the door frame of Macy's office. "I'm running down to the diner to get a cheeseburger and some caffeine. Do you want anything?"

Turned out Amanda was a darn good writer. She made a lot of grammatical errors, but those were easy to correct. Teaching someone to have a voice that comes through in his or her writing was something else.

Amanda had it, and had created a column geared for students. It covered everything from homework tips to saving for proms to how to graduate without a load of debt. She referenced students of all ages and backgrounds, and even added personal tidbits from things that her family did and said.

"Yes, if you don't mind. And I'll treat."

Sweets were necessary if she wanted to survive the afternoon. She might as well wallow and get fat since she had abysmal luck with men. And really, after all the friendly advice she was more confused than ever about what she should do.

"I'll take a cheeseburger, as well. But get me whatever kind of ice cream they have. If they have pints or whatever, that will work. I just need something gooey and full of sugar."

Amanda smiled. "Have you ever had the chocolate fudge ripple from Dory's Dairyland?"

She shook her head.

"I've got you covered. Oh, by the way, your friend—the hot marine—dropped this by." She handed Macy a flash drive.

Macy gulped hard. "Did he say anything?"

Amanda thought for a minute. "Just that this was a sample, and if you didn't like it you can email him with changes." She turned to walk away, and then stuck her head back in the office. "And, Harley. He said to tell her that he missed her. A lot."

With that, Amanda was gone.

"Hmm, at least he misses one of us," she said as she plugged the flash drive into the USB port.

I just wish it were me.

12

STAYING AWAY FROM Macy was slowly killing him. He'd peeked through the window at the paper and watched her as she worked on her computer. He felt silly, but he couldn't help it. Before she turned, though, and saw him, he rushed to the front door to go in and leave the flash drive for her. His mother's advice was to give Macy what she wanted. Time and space.

But he worried each day that the longer they were apart, the easier it would be for her to walk away from what they had.

And they definitely had something. It wasn't just about her being his. He knew that now. His pride had felt threatened that night, but it was more about him finding the thing that made him whole.

He hadn't slept much since they'd parted. She calmed him and being in her presence had become a sanctuary of sorts. He hadn't fully recognized all she'd done for him.

She was the first woman who knew him inside and out, and still accepted him. Wanted him, in fact.

Which was probably why her rejection had felt like a fatal blow.

His mother said it was only a rejection, but it still felt like life ending to him.

After parking his truck behind the feed store, he went straight to the room in back. His mom sat there, reviewing something on the computer.

Taken by complete surprise, he blurted out, "What are you doing here?" Try that again, he told himself. "I mean—"

"Momma D is feeling better, and she insisted I was cramping her style. I came back for a couple of days and then I'll go down on the weekend to check on her again. You look awful, son."

"Thanks, Mom."

His cell rang. He frowned.

"Who is it?"

"Her," he said.

"Quick, answer it before she hangs up."

Blake stared at the phone for another second, and pushed Answer. "Hello."

"Blake." Macy sounded as if she'd been crying. "I need you to come to the office right away."

"What's wrong? Are you hurt? Is it Harley?" He picked up the keys he'd thrown on the desk and turned without so much as a see ya to his mother.

She cleared her throat. "No, I'm sorry. I didn't mean to worry you, but this is time sensitive and I really need to see you now if you can make it."

"I'll be there in five."

He was there in four.

Striding in, he bolted straight past the receptionist, who didn't seem shocked to see him, and into
Macy's office.

She had her head down while petting Harley, who
was sprawled out on the floor. When the dog saw
him, she jumped up and then ran full force into him
knocking him into the chair.

"Harley! Down, girl! Blake, did she hurt you?"
Macy went to his side and grabbed the dog by the
collar. "Sit, Harley," she commanded.

Harley obeyed immediately but kept her attention
on Blake. He could have sworn she smiled at him, her
tongue hanging out of the side of her mouth.

"No, she's okay. Hey, girl," he said and affectionately scratched behind her ears. She nuzzled his
neck and he wrapped his arms around her. He'd truly
missed the giant horse of a dog. She proceeded to sit
in his lap like a human would and they nearly toppled
over backward.

"That's enough!" Macy exclaimed, waving at the
dog. "You really missed him, I get it. I missed him,
too. Now get off of him and get back to your spot.
Now."

Harley looked back at him.

"Better do what she says, girl."

The dog huffed and returned to her gel-pad dog
bed.

"Sorry about that. She's excited to see you."

Macy grabbed a tissue and dabbed her nose. He
remembered how she'd sounded on the phone. "Macy,
tell me what's wrong."

"Nothing's wrong. I mean, yes, there are some things we need to talk about but—these stories you wrote—"

She paused.

Something *was* wrong with them. "I told you I'm not a journalist." He wasn't upset. Maybe a bit disappointed. He'd enjoyed meeting and talking to past military personnel, especially the older vets from long ago.

"Not a journalist?" she scoffed and then smiled. "They're brilliant. Choked me up a little they were so good. There are a few style points I'll need to fix, but other than that, they're okay to print. That's why I called you. I'm going to pull the front page. I'd like to run the first two stories right now. And then, if you're up to it, make it a weekly series."

She liked what he'd done. "Uh, I'm not sure they're front-page worthy," he said, "but thanks."

"I'm the publisher, I decide what is worthy of the front page. And for the record, this has nothing to do with you and, well, what's been going on with us. I want to make that clear."

So it was just business. "Sure," he said. "Feel free to make the changes you think are necessary. I'm glad you liked the stories."

He stood.

"Where are you going?"

He frowned, confused. "Was there more?"

Standing, she walked over and shut the door and the blinds. "Sit down, Blake."

He sat.

She picked up the phone and dialed.

"Davis, I'm sending you new copy for the front page." She paused to listen. "Yes, I know we already did the front page. But I have something better. Make sure you and Sam both look at it, and then send it on to the printer."

She hung up the phone.

Her longs legs moved in front of him, and she sat down on the edge of her desk. She wore dark denims that hugged her hips and were tucked into those stiletto boots he loved. She leaned over and her shirt gapped slightly, giving him a glimpse of purple lace.

"Are you seeing someone else?"

His head popped up. "Why would you say something like that?"

She bit her lip. "You haven't even tried to talk to me since what happened the other night."

He leaned back so he could focus on her face, because her breasts were distracting him.

"That's what you wanted. You said things were going too fast and that I was possessive. Time and space apart, I believe, was mentioned. So I've been doing that."

Crossing her arms, she stared at him. "I meant in regard to that one night. I was embarrassed and hurt. By the next day I was over it. But you didn't answer my question. Are you seeing someone else?"

"Who would I see?" he asked incredulously. "You've ruined me for anyone else."

It was the truth. No way in hell would he ever feel about another woman what he did for Macy.

She gave him a Cheshire cat–like smile. Then she

bent over so her arms were on the arms of his chair, her breasts eye level.

"You're seducing me," he said gruffly.

"Maybe." She slowly leaned in and kissed him.

"What would convince you? This?" She nibbled on his ear.

He coughed and kept his hands at his sides.

She edged her knees on either side of his legs in the large leather chair. Her heat rubbed against his cock. "Or maybe this," she teased and tormented, as her hand went to the fly of his jeans.

Gently, he seized her wrist and stopped her. "Macy, I'm going to lose it right here and now if you don't stop." Then he pulled her to him and ravaged her mouth.

"Not here," he said when he finally let her go.

"Why not?"

"Because when we do this, I'm going to make you moan my name so loud that everyone in town will know what we're doing."

She cocked an eyebrow. "Well, then. I suppose we'd better hurry home. I only have about an hour before the final proofs are ready."

"No. We aren't rushing this again. I'm taking you on a date. We'll have a nice dinner and—" She rubbed her heat over his strained cock.

"Stop distracting me."

She pouted. "What other things are we going to do on the date besides eat? Because I have food at home we can cook. And a soft bed where you can make me moan all night long."

Pulling away from him, she stood. "Unless you're not up for it?"

He chuckled. "When you want something, it's no holds barred, isn't it?"

"It is. So, Marine, I see this going one of two ways. I can make love to you in the restaurant of your choice in front of the customers, or you can come to my place and we can negotiate further."

He swallowed hard. "Will those boots be part of the negotiations?" He had a vision of her with nothing on but those damn boots.

"They could be, but before you leave, there's one more thing."

"Anything you want, babe, it's yours."

"From now on, if we have a disagreement about the terms of our mutual companionship, we discuss it. Calmly. And if I say I need a little time, I'm talking hours—at the most, a night. Understood?" She knelt in front of him and unzipped his jeans.

"Yes," he groaned. "Macy, I'm never going to be able to walk out of here if you keep doing that."

"By my clock we have an hour to fill before I look at those final proofs, so we're going to have some fun."

Her head dipped down and she slid her tongue along his shaft.

"Macy," he said, gritting his teeth, "this feels, you fee…"

Pushing her hair away from her face, she stared up at him. "I know, Blake. I feel it, too."

Before he could say another word, her mouth was on him again.

13

HAVING HER COFFEE in the backyard while tossing a chew toy to Harley, Macy was at peace. Even happy, maybe. When had she ever been able to say that? She had a home that was hers, and a dog that she loved and who loved her. It was like a dream that was never within reach when she'd covered so many stories and crisscrossed the globe.

Most of her adult life had been lived around some conflict. Adrenaline-fueled jaunts pursuing one lead and then the next. She accepted that was how she would spend the rest of her days, knowing that life might be cut short because of the job.

But now—that was no longer true.

Spending time in Tranquil Waters, learning to fit in, the intimacy with Blake—not just the sex—was beyond anything she'd ever experienced. All of these connections made her realize there was so much more to life than adrenaline and airports.

After the sixth throw of the toy, Harley ambled up to her. Macy sat down in a padded deck chair. Even in November, the weather was warm enough that she could be outside in a sweater and still feel comfortable. The same couldn't be said of what it was like in Boston at this time of year.

Her phone buzzed in her pocket, Harley lay at her feet. The dog had short spurts of energy and then she was tired for eight hours.

"You're up early," she said to her friend.

"It's your fault." Cherie yawned.

"Why is that?"

"Your ex won't stop calling me. He has something urgent he needs to talk to you about. He insists you call him now. And I'm supposed to tell you that it isn't personal. It's job related."

Macy frowned. "I don't want to hear anything from him, job related or whatever."

"Seriously, you need to talk to him. *Opportunity of a lifetime* was just one phrase he used. Said he owed you, and this was the big one."

"Last time I saw him, I seem to remember his 'big one' entertaining an intern."

Cherie coughed. "Hold on there. You made a joke."

"I discovered I have a sense of humor, go figure."

"Oh, Macy. Your marine must be something special if he's loosened you up enough to make jokes."

"He is something special," she said wistfully.

"You don't even sound like your old self. I thought you'd signed off on men for good?"

"I did. I have no clue how long this is going to last with the marine, but it's intense. I've— No matter what happens, it will have been worth the broken heart— At least in this case I've learned something about myself and what I want in a relationship."

"You have fallen in the deep end without your water wings again."

Definitely. But she hadn't lied. Nothing about the past few weeks would change if she had a chance to do them over again. Except perhaps, the three days they'd been apart. She was still ticked over the time they wasted.

"I always did like to take risks."

"So when do I get to meet him? You can and you will send me a picture."

"I promise, soon." Part of her didn't want to share Blake, it was new and seemed almost too good to be true. "Listen, I need to get to the office."

"Fine. Don't worry about me. I'm just the one waking up at the crack of dawn to give you news of limitless opportunities."

Macy laughed.

"Please, by all that you hold dear, call your ex. I wouldn't put it past him to hop on a private jet and fly down there to speak to you in person."

Ugh. Something she definitely did not want.

"Fine. And you know, Cherie, you can block his calls."

Cherie grunted. "I did, and then he called my assistant, which is the only reason I'm awake before ten."

An hour later she was at the newspaper office. Harley was in her favorite spot sleeping. Deadline day was always a long one for Macy. She had to edit and design the pages and make sure everything was electronically delivered to the printer on time.

In spite of the pressure, the new staff and other changes had made a positive difference and everyone had settled into a comfortable routine.

"Hey, I'm going to do a latte run. Do you want a sandwich or something to go with yours?" Amanda asked. Today she wore a pair of dark jeans, cowboy boots and a T-shirt promoting a punk rock band that had seen better days—the shirt, not the band. At least the outfit was a step in the right direction and Macy wasn't blinded by the color choices.

Glancing at her cell phone she saw that it was almost lunchtime.

"Yes." She pulled cash out of her purse. "And get yourself and Lance something, as well."

"Do you mind answering the phones? Lance is upstairs installing the new computer equipment."

"Not a problem."

Harley barked. The dog grabbed her leash from its hook and sat expectantly in front of Amanda.

Amanda rolled her eyes but smiled. "Yes, you may come, but you have to stay by the bicycle rack and if you try to trip me to get the food this time, there will be no more walks for you."

"You don't have to take her with you. That's a lot to juggle."

"It's okay, I know she just gets excited and can't help herself. Besides, she's a guy magnet. Everyone wants to know what kind of dog she is, because she's so big."

Laughing, Macy followed them to the door.

She slipped her fingers around Harley's collar. The dog looked at her. "You behave, or no cookies for you tonight."

Harley did her signature move and cocked her head to one side.

"I mean it."

Harley grumbled, but licked Macy's hand.

The dog really did understand everything she said. It was spooky sometimes.

After washing her hands, she propped open her office door and the front door of the building so she could hear if someone walked in.

The phone rang as she was passing Amanda's desk.
"Tranquil Waters News."

"I thought you owned the paper, why are you answering the phones?" The smooth voice of her ex was unmistakable.

Figures. As soon as Amanda leaves he would call.

"The receptionist is grabbing lunch. I don't have time to talk. I'm on deadline for our pages."

"Please! Don't hang up." She couldn't remember when he'd last used the word *please*.

"Whatever it is, Garrison, it can wait until tomorrow." She reached down to disconnect the call.

"The Henderson Paper Group wants you to be the executive editor of their online editions," he said quickly. "Aaron Henderson asked for you specifically."

She couldn't believe it. When she'd decided she was tired of traveling, she'd wanted to make a name for herself as an editor. In the six months she was at the Boston paper, which was one of Henderson's largest papers, she'd noticeably improved its bottom line. After streamlining the editorial process, the quality of the information had increased, bringing in more subscribers and consequently more advertisers.

"Are you still there?"

"Yes," she whispered.

"Henderson wants you back and he's bumping you up to executive editor. You're a hot commodity. The different papers in the chain all want you, they're fighting over you. I nearly got demoted when you left, because you had created such a dynamic online version that we were making more money than all the rest of the papers in the group combined."

She hadn't known that, but it pleased her. It meant that people were still interested in hard news, and not just what kind of underwear a celebrity might be wearing.

"You've worked with Aaron, and he's been watching what you've done with the paper there in Texas. From what we can tell, you've increased the ad revenue and circulation. And even though it's a small area without a lot of big news, the quality of reporting is exponentially better that it was six months ago."

"Did you do this?" If this was some bizarre plan to get her back to Boston, she wasn't interested.

This was beyond her dream job. To have creative and editorial input on an entire newspaper chain's online components was incredible. It also pulled at her heartstrings. Journalism, and the way it was reported. Ethics was the one aspect she felt strongest about. Good, objective reporting was needed in the world and this would give her enough influence to make that happen.

"No. In fact, I'd suggested another candidate. But Henderson only wants you. As far as he's concerned, there are no other candidates. He's in New York tomorrow and wants to meet with you personally. By the way, that's where the job would be."

Aaron Henderson had been her first editor, the guy who believed she was tough enough to be a war correspondent when no one else would give her a chance. She owed him. Big.

"That's really short notice."

"I've been trying to get in touch with you for two weeks. Did Cherie tell you I called?"

"Yes, but I've been busy." That was true.

The very least she could do was hear Aaron out. And she had to admit that it was a bit of an ego boost that they'd been watching what she did with the local paper.

"There's a first-class ticket waiting for you, all you have to do is claim it. The flight is at nine tonight. Once you land, a car will pick you up and take you to the hotel. You'll meet with Aaron there at ten the next morning. Are you in?"

Was she? Glancing around her office, taking in all the little changes that now made it hers...she knew it would be difficult to walk away. And what about her relationship with Blake? He had said he didn't plan on living in the small town for the rest of his life, but would he want to live in New York?

Before she spoke to him about it, she wanted to

know the fine print of what she was being offered. Then she'd make a decision.

"Yes. I'm in."

BLAKE HELD THE papers in his hand. An honorable discharge. There was a time he thought he'd go all the way and retire, but he was excited about new possibilities.

One of which was his mutual companionship with Macy. The other was figuring out his place in the world. He'd invested in his friends'—Rafe and Will's—security business. Anytime he wanted to step into a corporate roll it was there for him. He was already the CFO of sorts, overseeing most of the financials.

It meant a fair amount of travel, but that wasn't so awful. If he settled in Tranquil Waters, he'd need to let his soul free now and again. This kind of job might be the perfect answer. They had asked him to take over the rescue-operations department, as well. He'd coordinate search-and-rescue missions, which was something he'd always wanted to do.

His phone played Macy's favorite song. "Hey, beautiful, what's up?"

"How did everything go?" She didn't sound her normal self. There was hesitancy in her voice.

"Great. I've got my papers in hand, and I just landed at the Austin airport. How is everything with you?"

There was a long pause.

"Something has come up and I need to go to New

York for a couple of days. I could put Harley in a kennel, but I'd rather not."

What was in New York? Obviously she'd tell him if she wanted him to know. He guessed whatever it was was personal given the stress in her voice.

"I'll take care of her. What time do you have to leave?"

"My flight is at nine tonight, so I'd like to get out of here by seven at the latest."

"I'll be there by three. Do you want me to keep her at Mom's?"

"Uh, if you don't mind staying here, that would be better for her, I think. But I don't want to put you out."

"You aren't. Is everything okay?"

Another long pause. "Yes. It's— I've got a lot to process in a very short amount of time. Can we talk about it when I get back? I'll know more about the situation, and—we'll figure things then. Okay?"

Figure what things out? She said "we," so she probably wasn't going back to the ex. Besides, he was in Boston. Was it something to do with a job? He knew if he pressed her for details she'd see it as prying, even though her curiosity about everything was boundless. Macy had a double standard when it came to her privacy.

"Whatever you want." He tried to keep the sting of hurt out of his tone. That she wouldn't share what it was she had to figure out bothered him. Hadn't she been the one complaining that he never opened up?

"I have to put the paper to bed, but then I'll be out at the house. Thank you. I'm sorry I won't get to spend time with you. I've missed you."

Well, there was that.

"I missed you, too," he said.

"Bad timing that I have to leave tonight, but it can't be helped. This— It just came up this afternoon." There was a wistfulness to her words that pleased him.

Why wouldn't she just tell him?

"It's okay. You can make it up to me when you return, which is when?"

"I would imagine late tomorrow night or early the next day. Everything is kind of up in the air. And I'm sorry to be so vague. But I'll know more soon.

"Oh, and can you pick up another bag of food for Harley from the feed store? I'd really appreciate it."

"No problem."

By the time he picked up the food and dealt with a few things at the store it was almost four before he pulled up in front of Macy's house.

A large bark came from the other side of the front door, followed by the rattling of the handle.

"Harley, you stop that. No more opening doors, you brat," Macy chastised.

He chuckled. The dog never ceased to amaze him.

"She's keeping you on your toes," he said as Macy opened the door for him.

Harley held out a paw and he shook it. Then she nuzzled his hand.

"I'm glad to see you, too, girl." He rubbed her ears.

"And you." He kissed Macy as they jointly leaned over the dog's head.

He ended the kiss, but she captured his neck in her hand and held him to her where her lips devoured his.

When she finally broke the embrace, she stared deeply into his eyes. A storm brewed there, but he couldn't get a read on her.

"Are you doing okay?" He shifted the dog out of the way so he could put an arm around Macy's shoulders.

"I am. I don't mean to be so secretive, it's just—it's a job thing. A dream job, to be exact. At least that was what the ex told me."

The ex. At the mention of him, Blake's lips tightened into a thin line. "I see."

She didn't seem to notice the tension he felt, which was good. His ego, where she was concerned, had very nearly cost him their relationship. He wouldn't go there again.

"Yes, that's why I have to go. I don't know if he's telling me the truth or not about this job. But it's working with someone I like a great deal, and who gave me my break in the business. I feel like I owe it to him to at least hear him out."

The ex, or someone else? He couldn't come up with a subtle way to ask, without sounding like a jealous boyfriend. They'd said from the beginning that this was a fling, even though it had come to mean a great deal more to him. But he was the last one to stand in the way of someone's dream. Whatever she decided, he cared for her enough that he would support her.

He was just grateful it was about a job, and not another man.

She moved away from him and headed for the bedroom. "I need to grab my carry-on, and then I'll—" She smiled sheepishly. "I was going to say I'd show you where everything is for Harley, but you know all of that as well as I do. The good news is I went on a cooking binge while you were gone. There's a bunch of stuff in the freezer, and I just put the King Ranch casserole in the oven. It needs to cook about twenty more minutes. The buzzer will ring."

"For someone who doesn't really cook, you've been doing a lot of it lately." He smiled.

"It's your fault, making me watch all those cooking shows. I get inspired and then I get in there and go crazy. It's one of the few ways I can settle my mind. I guess, like running, it's my kind of meditation, only a lot more fattening. As soon as my knee is back in shape, I'll have to start running again so that my clothes will fit."

At the mention of food, Harley barked twice. Her signal for feeding time.

He chuckled as he put his duffel bag on one of the bar stools. "I've got her food in the back of the truck, I'll go get it."

"There are a couple of cups left in the old bag, but not near enough for her nightly feast. And watch it if you eat apples, bananas or peanut butter. She'll leave the roasted chicken on the counter but put one of those down and it disappears in the blink of an eye."

"Noted. Do you need a ride to the airport?"

"Oh, thanks, but since it's such a fast turnaround, I'll just take my car."

"If you get your carry-on, I'll put it in the SUV for you."

She went to the bedroom and returned with the suitcase. Dressed in an ivory sweater, dark jeans and heeled boots, she took his breath away. Dammit. Whatever this business was, it was going to mess things up for them. He knew it instinctively.

And that hit him hard, as hard as any man could punch. He didn't want to lose her.

"What's wrong?" She touched his cheek with her fingertips.

"Not a thing. Though I'm worried slightly about you driving the hour into Austin. The traffic was a bear getting here, and you'll be right in the thick of it."

She kissed his cheek where her fingers had been. "You are the sweetest man ever. I'll be fine. Are you sure everything is okay with you? That was a big decision you made about taking the honorable discharge."

"A decision I'd been thinking about for the last six months or so. I'm good. Like you, I'm taking a look at my opportunities and trying to figure out my next move."

"I guess—it's good that we have so many opportunities. There are a lot of people who don't," she said.

"Yes, we're extremely lucky." He kissed her lightly on the lips. "Say your goodbyes to you know who. I'll go put this in the car for you."

Outside, he took a long breath.

Hell.

What if she got in that car and she never came back? It was hard for people to turn down dream jobs. She was talented, it was no wonder someone wanted her.

But no one wanted her more than he did.

Hauling the giant bag of dog food onto his shoulder, he grabbed the groceries he'd bought with the other hand.

When he got to the door, she was holding it open for him and trying to keep Harley inside. "Oh, I should have called and told you about all the food I'd made."

Once in the house, he set the giant bag next to the kitchen door.

"What? Oh?" He glanced down at his hand with the other bag. "These things aren't for me, they're ingredients for a new kind of dog cookie I wanted to try for Harley."

At the word cookie, the dog came sliding down the hall and stopped at his feet.

"She scares me sometimes," he said, nudging the dog out of the way so he could move things into the kitchen.

"You said it," she agreed. "I find myself being careful about what I say just in case I accidentally use one of her cues. But I swear she understands most of the English language." She sighed. "I guess if traffic is bad, I should get going."

He nodded regretfully.

Wrapping his arms around her, he kissed her.

Pressing her body into his, she intensified the exploration of tongues as if she were communicating something else, as well.

Before he could think too much about it, he was lost in her. Her touch did that to him.

They were panting when they finally separated.

"Never in my life has a man affected me the way

you do," she said softly. "And I don't just mean when we make love."

He sucked in a breath. He hadn't realized how much he needed to hear her say that. "The feeling's definitely mutual," he said.

"I don't want to go," she said softly. "I want to stay here with you."

"I want that, too. So hurry up and get back." He kissed her one more time.

Then he scooted her toward the front door and led her out to the car. Opening her door for her, he waited until she was belted.

"I have to kiss you one more time," he said.

"That's a good idea." She tilted up to meet his lips.

"Be safe."

She nodded and gave him a sweet smile. "Take care of my girl."

"Done," he replied, and he shut the door and waved.

Everything was about to change. He knew it in his bones. He waved again though her car was already where the driveway met the road.

Damn.

Harley whined beside him.

"I know, girl. I love her, too."

_14_

As MACY STEPPED out of the glass-and-marble shower in her hotel room, her phone beeped. Wrapping a towel around herself, she picked up the cell. A picture of Blake and Harley graced her screen. He had his fingers crossed, and the dog had one paw crossed over the other.

The text read, We're crossing fingers and paws that everything goes well for you today. No matter what happens, we are here for you.

The photo and message were the cutest things she'd ever seen and were exactly what she needed to help with jangled nerves.

The Henderson Paper Group had come to her, not the other way around, and besides, she didn't need the job. Still, she had a bad case of the jitters that the warm shower hadn't calmed.

Taking a deep breath, she texted back, You made my day. Thank you! I miss you!

For someone who didn't use exclamation points in her work, she meant every one of them today.

Do you have time for a call? he texted.

Hearing his voice would be the balm that she needed to make it through the next few hours.

Call me in ten minutes, she texted back.

Someone knocked on her door.

"Hold on," she called out as she yanked on the hotel robe and tied the belt around her waist.

Peeping through the peephole, she frowned.

"I know you're in there," Garrison said.

"Why are you here?" she asked through the door.

"Aaron wanted me to bring you to him. Thought you might be more comfortable if you showed up with someone you know."

"I'll be fine. Thanks, anyway. You can go."

"It won't look good. That is, it won't look good if we aren't playing on the same team. Your group will be answering to me. He needs to know we can get along."

Huffing, she opened the door.

The man always looked gorgeous in a suit. Nowhere as good as her marine, but he *was* a looker.

"Sit." She pointed to the sofa under the windows on the far side of the room. "Don't talk to me. Don't do anything. Just sit there until I get dressed." She scooped up her dress, tights and boots and headed for the bathroom.

Her phone rang as she was putting on her dress and she couldn't open the door.

Mortification set in when she realized Garrison had answered the call.

"She's getting dressed, who is this? What kind of

friend?" He sounded jealous when he had absolutely no right to be. That was so not what she needed.

Slamming the door open, she then rushed to grab the phone out of Garrison's hand.

"I told you to sit," she said, annoyed. She pointed to the sofa for emphasis.

He ignored her. "Sorry, I thought it might be the boss telling you the meeting was moved or rescheduled."

What a lie. He was just being nosy. You could take the reporter out of the newsroom and make him a vice president, but you could never take that need for information out of a journalist. That quest for knowledge never died.

"Blake?"

"Hey," he said hesitantly. "Everything okay there?"

"Yes, sorry. I was in the bathroom and someone decided he'd answer my phone, although I didn't ask him to. So, how are you and our girl?"

He chuckled. "I like that. A lot. We're good. She went for a fast walk with me, as fast as I could go with this leg, anyway. She's tuckered out and laying in front of the fireplace. She moved her sofa in front of it last night while I watched the game. I filmed it for you, but it's too big to text."

She laughed. That must have been a sight. "Oh, I really needed that. Thank you. Great Danes get cold. And their bones get achy. I bought some glucosamine tablets for her, but you have to coat the pills in peanut butter to get her to swallow them."

"Got it," he said.

"Uh, can I be the jealous boyfriend for a minute and ask who that guy was."

Get in line. On the one hand she didn't want Blake to get the wrong idea, but on the other hand she wouldn't lie.

"The ex. He's escorting me to the meeting. It's in the publisher's suite, so they wanted me to feel comfortable. Evidently." She moved into the bathroom when she spied Garrison listening to every word with a giant grin on his face.

"And are you more comfortable?"

She huffed and closed the door. "No. I'd rather not have to deal with him while I'm contemplating everything else that's happening. It's weird. I'm not angry anymore—just…irked because I don't like him much as a person."

Her marine let out a deep breath. "I have to admit, I'm glad to hear that. When he answered the phone—"

"I would have thought the same thing," she interjected. "But, trust me, you have nothing to worry about."

"Time to go," Garrison called to her.

"I heard him," Blake said. "Whatever happens today I support you and so does Harley. Right, girl?"

Harley barked in agreement.

That Blake was so supportive brought tears to Macy's eyes. Most of the men in her past were too competitive to be truly supportive, including Garrison. It wasn't until after she'd broken up with him that she'd seen their relationship had become a game of one-upmanship.

"I wish you were here with me," she whispered, not bothering to keep the want from her voice.

"Ditto, babe. Ditto. Call us and let us know how it went."

"Will do."

As she hung up, she heard Harley bark again.

She loved that damn dog.

And she loved the marine.

Settling down in a small town with them didn't seem like such a wild notion to her.

But the opportunity from Aaron tugged at her. A real chance to make her mark in this environment was so enticing. Still, she first had to listen to what he had to say.

She marched forward and opened the bathroom door. "Right. Let's do this."

"Uh. You might want to put shoes on." Garrison raised his eyebrow.

"Well spotted," she said with dripping sarcasm. "He does that sort of thing to me."

"*He* being the boy back home?" Garrison asked.

"He's a man—a decorated marine to be exact—and yes. Not that it's any business of yours."

"Ah. The lady is a little testy. Was he jealous about your ex answering the phone?"

"He has nothing to be jealous about."

Minutes later, they'd left her room and were in the elevator, heading for Aaron. Garrison used a key card in a slot beneath the row of elevator buttons, he pushed the *P* for penthouse.

They want me.

No need to be worried.

On the short flight up, she realized why she was worried. She was about to get the job of a lifetime, one she'd always wanted.

But there might be a big sacrifice in store for her to take the position.

No. I can't think about that right now.

Just listen to what the man has to say.

Then you can make an informed decision.

As the elevator doors opened, she steeled herself. Plastering a smile on her face, she left the elevator and approached the penthouse door.

This was it.

"You look beautiful," Garrison said behind her. "In fact, your small-town life seems to agree with you."

Forcing herself not to roll her eyes, she raised her hand to knock on the door.

"Say anything like that when we're in there, and you'll really regret it." She had no desire to deal with his games and meaningless flirtations.

"You were always a fierce one," he whispered in her ear. "And one of the biggest mistakes of my life was letting you go."

"You didn't let me go. I ran as fast as I could from your toxic, cheating self, which was one of the best things I've ever done. I've met a man's man, one who honors and respects me. A man who deserves me."

"Sounds boring."

She laughed. "Not even a little bit. He's taught me a lot about my body, enough that I know what I've been missing out on all these years."

She glanced back to see his eyes narrow.

Not her finest moment, to throw such a comment

at him, but maybe she'd save the next poor woman he got together with. Everything had always been about his pleasure.

Jerk.

The door opened and Aaron Henderson ushered her in. She'd been expecting one of his aides to answer and she nearly tripped as she passed by him. He steadied her and then guided her to a sofa in the living room.

"I'm so glad you're here," he said. Dressed in gray slacks and a cream shirt, he looked the epitome of classy casual. But she knew how hard he'd worked to own his newspaper group. At forty-five he'd accomplished more than most people did in double the years. "Can I get you some coffee?" He gestured toward a small tray on a table in front of the sofa.

"No, thank you." Her nerves were jittery enough.

"I'll leave you two to your meeting," Garrison said.

"No, please I'd like you to stay." Aaron nodded to a chair.

Aaron sat in the one opposite her.

Her ex hesitated for a moment, but then took one of the leather chairs to the side of the conversation area.

"Before I explain why I called you here, though I'm sure Garrison has mentioned a part of it, I need to know something. It's a touchy subject, but the truth is important to me if we're to move forward with this arrangement. It's personal and not something an employer would ever ask in the normal course of things. But this is a big step, so we need to be clear."

What the heck was he talking about? There was

nothing she couldn't answer. And Garrison didn't need to be here. What arrangement?

"I'll answer whatever it is," she said, defiant.

"Good. So explain to me why you broke your engagement to Garrison and ran off to the country to run your uncle's paper."

Crap.

AFTER MAKING SURE Harley was settled in the office at the feed store with his mother. Blake headed out to the barn where they kept the hay and fertilizers.

"Hey, Blake," Ray said. "What are you doing out here?"

He shrugged. "Need to work off some energy. Thought I'd help you with the bales."

The other man nodded. "Glad to have the help, but is your leg going to be okay?"

Blake patted his right thigh. "It likes a good workout now and then."

Sliding on his leather gloves, he picked up the first bale and walked it into the barn. After creating a stack of about ten, he worked on the next one.

What if she took the job? And really, why wouldn't she? From what her ex had told her, it was all of her dreams tied into one neat package. If she had to move to New York, what would she do with Harley?

What would she do with him?

No way could he lose her.

He could follow Macy, but would she want him to?

When her ex had answered the cell earlier, he was suddenly so angry. It scared him that his temper rose that quickly. That wasn't him.

You're jealous.

Hell. He'd never been jealous before the night of Jaime's party. He'd dated and even had a few girlfriends. But nothing like the connection he had with Macy. In such a short time she'd become everything to him.

He lived his days trying to find ways to please her and make her smile. And darn if that didn't make him feel good, as well. Being around her was the best therapy there was. She made him laugh and look at the world through her curious eyes. Having seen more than his fair share of the dark side of things, he'd become jaded.

The past few weeks, she'd shown him that yes there was darkness, but there was also light. Her articles and features about the local folks had warmed his heart. She understood the true essence of people.

She'd gone a step further and shared some of the stories of people she had met during her travels. Many of them had the same problems as folks here in a small Texas town. Ultimately, they all wanted the world to be safe for their children, put food on the table and have a decent roof over their heads.

No longer did he think of people as us and them. There were evil people in the world, but there were a lot of good people, too. People he would gladly die to protect. When he was in the thick of it, he hadn't been able to see the truth.

Macy wrote that the world was a melting pot and that everyone was more the same than they were different.

That was one of the ideals she could pursue on a

higher level if she took the job. He knew that before she had any of the details. She had a voice that should be heard, and he would not in any way hinder that.

"Not sure what those bales of hay have done to you, but throwing them around is getting messy," Ray's voice cut through his thoughts.

Blake's eyes took in the chaos around him. Two of the bales had busted and there was hay all over the floor.

"Sorry," he said as he reached for the broom. "I'll clean it up."

"Don't worry about it. Let's get the rest of these bales into the loft. It looks like it's about to rain. Mind if I hand them up to you?" Ray asked.

Stepping up on the ladder, Blake climbed into the loft. A half hour passed before the storm hit, and water poured down on the tin roof of the barn. Normally, it was a comforting sound.

But his mood was no better than it had been before he'd started. Though, his muscles certainly ached now. He'd be lucky to get out of bed in the morning.

"Go on," Ray coaxed him. "I'll clean this up. I'm betting that horse of a dog of yours is giving your mom hell about the thunder."

Damn. He'd forgotten about Harley and loud noises.

Running through the rain and into the back of the store, he slid to a stop outside his mother's office door. She sat on the floor reading a book to the dog.

Blake chuckled. She'd done the same for his little brother who'd missed being struck by lightning by mere inches when he was six, and had been afraid of storms most of his childhood.

The crazy thing was the dog hung on her every word.

"Go check on Tanya at the register. There's news the river might flood. Folks will be stocking up. I'll be there once I get her to sleep." She rubbed Harley's head.

He nodded. Still soaked to the skin, he found Tanya had a long line in front of her.

Entering his code, he quickly opened the second register. "Next in line, please."

Grateful for the distraction, Blake's mind never wavered far from what Macy might be doing. Would she go out with the ex to celebrate?

Stop it. He forced himself to smile as he rang up the total for the nails and plastic tarp old Mr. Davis was buying. He did the same for all of the following customers, too. After the initial rush, the crowd thinned out.

He went to the office to check on his mom and the dog.

"You go ahead and take the dog home. She'll be more comfortable in a familiar place," his mom said.

The dog's head was in her lap on top of the small pillow his mother used for her back when she sat in the office chair too long.

"She looks pretty comfortable to me." He smiled.

She smiled back. "Yes, but my legs are numb from her overly large head, and I'm too old to be sitting on the floor."

After scooting the sleeping dog off his mom, he helped her up.

She stretched. "That's a smart dog you have there."

"That she is."

"For a monster, she kind of grows on you."

He laughed. At the sound, Harley glanced up and gave him the evil eye for waking her from her nap.

"Yep. She's too smart for her own good."

"Well, then. You two should get along just fine," his mom said as she patted his shoulder. "Any ideas on what your next move is? Are you sure you don't want to buy the store? You'd mentioned it when you were in the hospital, but we haven't talked about it since you got back."

That was before he met the woman who'd come to mean everything to him. And he'd also been told there was the possibility that he might not be the same again physically.

That wasn't an option for him, and he'd shown everyone, including himself, that he refused to allow his injuries to dictate the rest of his life.

"While you're gone, Mom, I do enjoy hanging out here, but this is your passion. I think mine is elsewhere. The guys have asked me to take a more active part in the security firm. They have some new ideas that might be beneficial to rural areas especially. So I'll probably be helping them grow the business. As soon as I know my next step, you'll be the first one I tell," he promised.

Giving him the mom-knows-all stare, she said, "You haven't heard from her yet, have you?"

"Mom," he warned.

"Son, I'm not saying anything except that her meeting was this morning and it's nearing five."

"I'm aware. Let it go—please."

She shrugged. "Whatever you say. I'll go help Tanya close up. You're soaking wet, get home before you catch your death."

Home. It hit him that it was Macy's house where he now felt at home.

Yes, ma'am. He was in big trouble.

15

As he braked in the driveway and put the truck into Park, Harley woofed. "Let me turn off the engine at least." He patted her back. As soon as he opened his door and got out, she leaped past him and ran for the house.

She must be hungry.

The dog opened the front door before he could get there. That wasn't right. He was certain he'd locked the door when they left earlier in the day.

"Hello, pretty girl. I missed you, too," Macy said as she greeted Harley. "I was a little concerned about you two. I tried to call, but no one answered."

She glanced up at Blake. He could see the concern on her face.

"You called my cell?" He went to take the phone out of his pocket, and discovered it wasn't there. "Well, that explains it," he said. "I must have lost it when I was working with Ray in the barn this afternoon."

Harley soon had her pinned against the fridge demanding to be fed. He grabbed the towel he'd left by the garage door and wiped the rain off of the dog's coat before she ruined the sexy dress Macy wore. She had on high-heel boots, and her hair was done up in that haphazard way that made her look like the sexy librarian.

Though, they'd never had a librarian in Tranquil Waters that ever looked like that.

"I missed you," she said. There was something in her expression that he couldn't quite understand.

"And I missed you. I'm surprised you're here."

"Where else would I be?" She smiled but it didn't quite meet her eyes.

Hell. She was going to take the job.

She held up a hand. "I haven't made a decision yet," she said as if she could read his thoughts. "In fact, I don't want to think about anything right now. The flight into Austin was one of the bumpiest I've ever been on, and I've flown on a lot of planes. Then the traffic this time of day getting out of Austin through the rain was enough to turn me into one of those road-rage maniacs. I could never understand how people got so angry in the car, but I do now.

"All I want is a hot bath and a glass of wine, and I want you to join me."

His body was instantly at attention. Who was he to question if she needed some time?

"Red or white?" he asked. He had a bottle of champagne in the fridge, which he planned to surprise her with if she took the job. But now wasn't the right moment.

"You pick. And do we have any chocolate? I really, really, really need chocolate."

He laughed. "You go start the bath. I'll bring in the treats."

"Deal," she said. "Come on, Harley, have a seat on the couch. *Bad Dog!* is just starting."

"Make sure it's not one of the animal rescue episodes. It upsets her when she sees other animals in pain," he said. He'd made that mistake the night before and ended up sleeping next to her on the floor. It was the only way she'd calm down.

"I should have told you about that. In my rush, I must have forgotten."

As he opened the cabernet sauvignon, he tried not to think about Macy. But he knew the truth.

Finding the box of chocolate truffles he'd bought for her to celebrate, he placed them and the wine on a serving tray he found next to her fridge.

As he passed Harley on her couch she glanced up at him. "Tell you what? You stay there for the next hour or so and behave, and I'll give you two more of these." He put a dog cookie down in front of her. Harley cocked her head and he swore she winked at him. Then she settled back on her sofa to watch her favorite channel.

Balancing the wine, glasses and chocolates again, he found Macy already to her neck in bubbles.

He placed the drinks and plate on the small round table next to the tub and poured the wine.

Handing her the filled glass, he smiled when she moaned with the first sip. His cock twitched, as well. Indeed, one small moan and he was hard.

"Are you sure you want to share the bath, you look pretty comfortable."

She reached out and tugged on his jeans. "Hey, these are already wet."

"I suppose you may not have noticed, but it's raining outside, and wrestling with your dog to get her into the truck was no easy feat. I am grateful that the thunder had stopped by the time we got home. I had to tell her a story on the way as she tried to hide from the noise.

"What kind of story?" She pointed to his shirt as if to say, "Hurry up and strip," so he did.

Her eyes followed him appreciatively as he slid into the tub across from her. Even with his size, he could stretch out his sore legs. His body warned there'd be a steep price to pay for lifting all those bales of hay.

"Mom watched her while I was out in the barn. When I came back, she was reading a romance novel to her. Harley hung on her every word. I swear she understood her."

Macy popped a chocolate in her mouth, and then she shook her head. "I'm not surprised. She's so smart. Sometimes I forget that she's a dog. I talk to her like I would any friend."

"If it makes you feel any better, I do the same thing. But don't tell anyone I said that."

She watched him for a moment from under her lashes. "Tell me about your day," she said before having a large sip of wine.

As he shared the minute details, she shifted around so that she rested against his chest. His legs stretched out along hers, his hard cock pressing into her back. He put his arms around her and drew in her scent.

She was his.

No matter what she told him, he had to find a way to stay in her life. Compromise wasn't one of his strong suits, but he could learn if it meant being closer to her.

"Weren't you afraid of hurting your leg?" she asked.

"Huh." Then he remembered what he'd been telling her about loading hay into the barn. "No. It's good to work out once in a while and push harder than I normally do. Helps build up strength." At least that was what his PT had told him a few months ago.

"So you're feeling okay?" As she asked she turned to face him. She was on her knees, the bubbles creating a pretty swirling design across her breasts.

"Right now, I feel great," he said as he reached out and rubbed his thumb across one of her taut nipples. It hardened even more at his touch.

"I need you," she whispered.

Not nearly as much as he needed her. Leaning down, he teased her sensitive skin with his tongue.

She hissed in a breath.

"I've wanted you since I heard your voice on the phone this morning," he said and raised his head to kiss her. As his tongue played with hers, his fingers found her sex. He stroked her until she arched back and cried out.

"Yes," she moaned. "Yes."

Then she gently moved on top of him.

He shifted forward so she could wrap her legs

around him. She gripped his shoulders as she rode him, his arms strained to keep them as one.

Their bodies rose and fell, and the water sloshed around them. The overwhelming sensations as he filled her had him gritting his teeth for control.

"Please, Blake. Don't hold back. I want to feel all of you."

He smiled and upped their rhythm. He savored every word, every sound that came from Macy's lips.

Throwing her head back, her face radiant, her body began to quiver. Her muscles tightened around him as the orgasm rocked her, and he could hold on no longer.

"Mine," he whispered fiercely as he climaxed.

"Yes," she said. Her lips on his.

When he tilted her forward, so he could see her eyes, a tear streamed down her cheek.

"What is it baby? What's wrong?"

Chewing on her lip, she shook her head.

"You took the job." It was more of a statement than a question.

"Not yet. I— We need to— What we have is so intense. I don't think I can live without it. We said that this was a fling. That we weren't serious."

"We ran past serious the first night we made love," he said as he moved a damp curl from her eyes.

"I thought so, too. That's why I don't want to make this decision, and it really is a life-changing one, without discussing it with you. I have no right…"

He smiled. "I love you, Macy," he told her. "I'm with you no matter what you choose to do."

It took a minute for his words to register. "I love

you, too." She put her arms around his neck and hugged him. "This is strange, right? We've only known each other a few weeks."

He agreed. "But I don't think that's anything we can control."

She shivered.

"Let's move to where it's comfortable," he said. "I think this conversation is going to need more wine, and maybe some of that casserole you made."

She frowned. "Except for the chocolates and wine, I haven't been able to eat all day," she said as he helped her up and into the large walk-in shower. The glass curved so that there was no need for a door.

"Well, no decision should be made on an empty stomach—at least that's what my mom always says." As the warm water sluiced down their bodies, he gathered her close to him. "We will figure this out. I promise."

She smiled and squeezed him tight. "Why does life have to be so hard?"

He kissed the top of her head. "Got to get through the bad to get to the good," he told her. And he meant it.

Could he support her if she went off to New York and left him and Harley behind? It was no place for a dog as big as she was.

It wasn't lost on him that he was prepared to sacrifice a great deal for that damn dog—and even more so for the woman in his arms.

AFTER A GOOD MEAL, which Blake insisted Macy eat, they snuggled on the couch. Automatically, she changed the channel to Nova. The dog watched entirely too much television, but she'd probably done so with her former owner.

There had been times when the television popped on while Macy had been in the bath, or outside in the backyard or garage. And the channel always seemed to land on one of Harley's favorites. When Macy arrived back in the room, the dog would look around as if she had no idea how it had happened.

"This is where I want to be," she said. "Next to you, with the dog watching our favorite shows. Well, her favorite shows." She grinned as she looked up at him.

"I'm kind of fond of our time together, as well," he said. "But being comfortable isn't the same thing as being happy. I care for you too much to let you turn down a lifelong dream."

She gathered her knees up under her and rested her chin on them. Could she handle a new relationship, and a very time-consuming job? What would she do with Harley? The thought of giving her up was just impossible. She loved the dog.

"Tell me what the job entails."

She explained that she would be in charge of all of the online components for the publishing group's papers. They would use a specific strategy to grow their online content, and use a more uniformed format. She'd have almost a hundred people on her staff located across several countries. Henderson wanted to bring her old-school principles to their online content, which was sorely needed.

Stories went up too fast, a lot of facts went unchecked. They'd all agreed, after the very uncomfortable conversation about her ex and why she left, that it was time for them to create a place in Henderson Newspaper Group where people could go to find solid journalistic principles and legitimate stories online, in a timely manner.

Blake whistled and put a hand on her shoulder. "That's impressive. And you have to know it's a huge honor that they think so much of you."

She nodded. Her ego, in between bouts of bone-crushing insecurity, had been buffed more than once during the meeting in New York. She questioned whether she was up for the job, but they believed in her so much that she stopped doubting herself. "Yes. But I'm really torn. I love the life I've created here with you and Harley. The town has even begun to accept me. And I feel like I've made a real difference with the paper."

"True, though now you can take your plans and strategies and ideas out to the wider world," he encouraged. "Talk about making a difference."

She cocked her head to the side and glared at him. "I want you to say, 'you can't leave. You're my woman.' All cavemanlike." She frowned.

"I will, if that's what you actually want. But what kind of man would I be if I kept you from fulfilling your dreams?"

"The kind of man I usually fall for," she snorted. "Many guys wouldn't want their significant other running off to parts unknown to manage a company—at least, part of it, that is."

"Macy, if we've learned anything over the last few weeks, it's that there's nothing *usual* about us."

"You're right." She imitated her receptionist's gesture and bumped fists with him.

He chuckled, but it wasn't a happy sound.

"This relationship is just beginning," he said. "We fell fast for one another. But maybe, like you said, it's good that we slow down to figure out what we want to do next. I'm not sure myself. Moving to New York would be somewhat easy for me, since I own part of a security firm there. But I feel like my next step should be my own."

"So you think it would be good for us to be apart?" She chewed on the inside of her lip.

He frowned at her. "No. I can't stand the idea of being away from you, but I think it's important that you at least try to do this. Dreams change, but this kind of opportunity is something that you've been dedicated to for a long time. There will be serious regrets if you don't get out there and give it a chance."

She sighed. "Why do you have to be so smart *and* handsome?"

He gathered her into his lap. "You're the good-looking one. I'm going to check into chastity belts online. You can find almost anything on the internet these days."

She sputtered and laughed. "Trust issues, dude. Trust issues."

He winked at her.

"There's only one man allowed to touch me," she whispered as she kissed his neck.

"And who's that?"

"A certain marine who has me going every which way so that I'm constantly confused."

He tapped her chin with his fingertip. "Hey, I'm trying to make this easy on you."

She put her palms to his chest. "It would be easier if you'd just tie me to the bedpost and make me a kept woman."

"Hmm." He looked as if he were genuinely contemplating the idea. "I didn't know you were into that, but I'm sure we could work something out."

Suddenly, she hopped from his lap.

A moment of clarity hit her. "I'm scared," she said.

"You wouldn't be human if you weren't," he spoke softly.

"No, not about the job. About losing you." How long would he wait while she was supposedly achieving her dreams?

"Hey, I'll be here. And maybe at some point I'll join you. That is, if we can sort out what to do with you know who."

Macy's heart jumped to her throat. She'd momentarily forgotten about Harley, she'd feel awful leaving the poor dog behind. They really had become family.

"That's going to be hard. I don't think there's a dog park big enough in the city to contain her."

"Well, you won't have to worry about it for a few months. Take the job, and give yourself time to get settled. Once things are in order, then we'll discuss what happens next for us."

"You always say you aren't so great with compromises," she said as she kissed the stubble on his chin. "And yet, you're a lot better at them than I am."

"Only when it comes to you. So, are you going to call Henderson?"

She shrugged. "I will call him, but not tonight. This is our time, yours and mine. His newspaper can wait. In fact, I have until Friday to let Aaron know of my decision and I'm going to take those days. Once I say yes, things will move very fast."

"We have two whole days?" His eyebrows waggled. She didn't have the heart to tell him that a lot of those hours would be spent trying to make sure she had the Tranquil Waters paper seen to. She wouldn't allow it to fail, especially since they'd all worked so hard. Her gut churned. There was so much here that she'd have to leave behind now.

Blake might believe her mind was made up, but she wasn't so sure. There had to be another answer, she was just too tired and wired to think clearly.

"Yes!" she said and kissed him smack on the lips. "So have your wicked, wicked way with me, Marine."

"How about those ropes and bedposts you were talking about," he joked and sent her a naughty grin.

"Oh? What would your mother say?"

"Are you going to tell her?"

She lifted her T-shirt over her head. "Do I look like a girl who would kiss and tell?"

And with that, she was lost in the sweet company of the man she loved.

16

WHEN HE JOINED the marines any hint of a distracting emotion was driven out of him. The words, "Separate yourself from the situation and get the job done," had been seared into his brain.

But that concept wasn't working so well today. While Macy packed, he'd made her eggs, bacon and waffles. He'd taken Harley out for a walk, and added a new playlist to her phone.

He did these things to keep his mind off the fact that in ninety minutes he'd be driving her to the airport, and there was every chance it'd be a month, maybe more, before he could see her again. The gnawing in his gut reminded him of those timely words from the military, even though he was trying to ignore the raw tension.

Whenever his brain began playing the what-if game, he occupied his mind by thinking of other gifts Macy could unwrap when she got to New York. She'd been given a corporate apartment in a fancy building with a doorman, so at least her place would have proper security. And Henderson had insisted she accept the car and driver he provided. He didn't want her wasting valuable time in the subway tunnels with no internet. The car had been specifically outfitted to be a mobile office for her. In the first few weeks she's be traveling to New Jersey, Upstate New York, Virginia and D.C., and after her most recent flight home, she wasn't thrilled about all the travel.

Henderson arranged for the car, and told her when she had to go to the Midwest and Pacific Northwest, she'd have use of the company jet. She had her boss on speakerphone when all of this was discussed, so Blake couldn't help but listen in. He'd never seen someone's eyes almost pop out of their head, but hers were close.

"So, Ms. Corporate Executive how does it feel to be traveling in style?" he asked after she hung up.

"Weird. I'm used to being the one in the middle seat in coach between the lady with the snotty two-year-old and the guy who's decided to be my new best friend on a fourteen-hour flight because the paper didn't have it in the budget and my reservation was made at the last minute. I've been in a jeep with no air-conditioning outside of Iraq when it was nearly a hundred and twenty degrees. There was about two years early in my career, when I didn't come back to the States. I existed with two pairs of khakis, four T-shirts and one pair of boots. I'd start every day not knowing where the story might take me. I usually had to bum rides and barter for taxi rides.

"So yes, it's weird." Then she'd taken his hands in hers. "Everything is changing so fast."

He'd kissed her fingers and smiled, even though it was forced. "Yes, but we have each other. And we're good."

She looked as if she were searching for courage. "I've never really had someone I could depend on before. It's—hard for me to—"

"Trust," he finished her sentence.

She nodded.

"After what you went through before you came here, it's understandable. But you have to realize, I come from a mind-set that we are a team. Harley and I are here for you. We'll video chat and text. And we'll both be so busy we won't even notice how long we've been apart."

"Do you genuinely believe that last bit?"

"No. But we can pretend our hearts aren't breaking while we're apart." He'd taken her in his arms. "There's a lot going on here, as well, but I'll find a way to come see you."

As it had done so many times in his life, opportunity was knocking. When he talked to Rafe and Will a few days ago he'd learned about their new idea that involved protection for wireless service in rural areas.

Their strategy was attractive to him, especially after listening to a frustrated Macy grumble about bad connections and loss of online access.

"Promise to never leave Harley on her own?"

He laughed. "Wherever I go, she does. I don't think I'd have a choice. We've seen what she does when she wants something."

"It's a big responsibility to dump on someone," she said guiltily. "I'm the one who adopted her."

"You did, and she's grateful. And I have lots of dog sitters if I ever need a break, though I doubt that will happen. We've become pretty good friends."

Macy snuggled into his chest. "Hold me really tight," she said.

He did.

She kissed him hard. "You are the most thoughtful man. And I saw the songs you added to my phone. I'm going to cry all the way to New York."

He stroked her back and recognized her sweet scent again. Though he doubted he'd ever forget it.

"I don't think I can do this," she choked out.

A lump of emotion sat in his throat. He swallowed hard, it didn't work. "You can, and you will. When you get scared, call me or focus on the adversity you've known in the past and overcome."

Her exploits seemed legendary to him. He had such respect for her and he knew she felt the same about him.

"Got your bags, ready to go?"

There was a tiny sob against his shirt.

Damn. He was just grateful it wasn't him doing the crying.

"Hey," he murmured, and he affectionately tapped her chin.

"I feel like I'm abandoning both of you," she said, glancing down at the dog. Harley was never more than two feet away from Macy since she'd brought her suitcases out of the closet.

"No. Don't think of it like that. You're going on your best adventure yet. You live for that sort of thing.

You'll call us each night and tell us about everything that happened, and we'll do the same."

Her phone rang. She handed it to him, too choked up to answer.

"Hello?"

"I'm calling for Ms. Reynolds," a man stated.

"Yes, she's indisposed at the moment, can I help you?"

"This is Mr. Henderson's assistant. He has sent the jet to pick her up so that she doesn't need to fly commercial. The plane is at a small private airfield about four miles outside of Tranquil Waters. The thing is, it's there now, waiting for her. So if she wouldn't mind bumping up her schedule to accommodate—"

The assistant left the rest up to him to decipher.

"We'll get her there as soon as possible."

"I'll text the address," the assistant said and hung up.

"Macy, there's good news and bad news," he told her. "The good news is you don't have to worry about any plane with crying babies or folks who want to adopt you. The bad news is that Henderson's jet is waiting for you out at the Jones airstrip. They'd like you to leave right now."

Her eyes flashed big. "But—but I'm not ready. I wanted to stop by the paper and make sure—"

"The gang has it handled and I'll be checking in with them often. Come on. I'll get your cases. We'll bring Harley with us."

A half hour later they drove straight up to the plane in his pickup. The sleek jet was luxurious and impressive.

The pilot met them at the door, and the steward took her luggage to stow in the back. The interior had rich leather seats and the walls had dark wood paneling. It reminded Blake of the exclusive club in London where he and Rafe had had Will's bachelor party. Coincidentally, the club wasn't far from his soon-to-be-wife's modeling show. They'd given him a hard time about modeling the jeans in the finale of her show, but he'd said there was nothing he wouldn't do for his woman.

At the time, Blake hadn't understood Will, but he did now. He would do anything for the woman he'd followed into that jet. Harley barked at the bottom of the steps. She and Macy had already said their good-byes. She was probably worried he was leaving, too.

"Wheels up in ten," the pilot said. "There's a storm brewing over the Atlantic, and we want to get you there before it hits."

That was the last thing poor Macy needed to hear.

"Sit here," he encouraged, and she claimed one of the cushy chairs. Her pink cheeks had gone pale at the mention of the storm. "You're going to be fine. You'll get there before the storm, that's why you have to leave now."

"It's going to be okay," she said as if she were trying to convince herself.

"I love you," he said as he knelt down on his good knee.

"I love you, too." She gathered his hands in hers, and he passed the small gift into her palm.

"What's this?" She opened her hand and revealed a silver chain with four charms on a ring.

"The Great Dane charm is self-explanatory. The saber represents me. The typewriter—I looked for a computer but they didn't have one—represents you. And then the heart is us." He turned the heart over so she could read the inscription. "'You are mine.'" He slipped the necklace over her head.

"This way, we'll always be with you, no matter where you are."

Tears streamed down her cheeks. She threw her arms around him and kissed him.

"This is the nicest, most beautiful gift anyone has ever given me," she croaked.

The tears were almost his undoing.

"I got you something," she said and dug into her tote bag. Holding out a small package, she handed it to him. "You've been so wonderful. It's not much, but— Just open it." She smiled through her tears and put the handkerchief he'd handed her to her nose.

"You didn't have to do this," he said as he ripped off the navy-and-red paper. Inside he found a scuba watch. It was the exact one he wanted. He'd been planning on replacing the one he'd broken when he was injured. He just hadn't gotten around to it.

"Read the inscription on the back." She grinned.

"'You are mine,'" he read out loud and then he chuckled.

"Great minds, right?" She laughed, but it sounded weak to his ears. He smiled, anyway.

"You're amazing. I love you so much," he said.

"Five minutes," the captain called to them.

"I better get going. I don't want Harley to hear the engines."

She frowned. "Yes, she won't like that at all. I don't want you to go."

He cupped her chin in his hand and kissed her lightly. "I don't want to, either, but it's okay. Now that we know we have each other."

He held up the watch. "Call me when you land."

She nodded, the tears falling faster down her cheeks.

The jaded journalist never cried, so he had a good idea how much this parting hurt her.

"I love you," she repeated as he headed to the exit.

"Be safe, you're my heart." Then he turned quickly so she wouldn't see the hurt in his eyes. She seemed to read him so well.

Is this what love did to people? Because it was painful.

Took everything he had to walk away from her when she was like that.

Harley whimpered as he hit the last step.

The plane made a high-pitched whining sound.

"Let's go girl, we have to be a safe distance away."

The dog didn't hesitate. She jumped into the cab of his truck. Then her paw pushed the button to close up the passenger-side window.

Backing the truck up first, he then drove out onto the dirt road that lead to the small airstrip.

The ground vibrated as the jet rumbled to life and soon gathered speed down the runway.

Harley barked as the jet was lost in the cloud cover.

"I feel the same way," he said.

Obviously pouting, the dog rested her jowls on the front dash.

"She'll be back." At least he hoped so.

He hadn't lied; it did feel as if his heart was flying away to New York City. He wasn't sure how he'd live without it.

17

FRIDAY COULD NOT come soon enough, although Macy had to work through the weekend, she could do most of it in her apartment. She'd forgotten what a rush a busy newsroom could be, but it was also draining.

Her team had accomplished a great deal in a short amount of time. The first two days, she put together a top gang of editors, columnists and reporters. Not one of them had turned down the opportunity when she explained her mission.

Not a single one. Jobs were scarce, but it was clearly more than that.

"This could revitalize the industry," her friend Jill, had said. They'd worked together to cover stories in Pakistan and Afghanistan. "Everyone will want in."

Jill was right. If Macy had any doubts about what they were doing, they were gone. By Thursday, she had a long list of everyone she wanted on her team. Most of them had to give two weeks notice, but luckily enough some of them were between jobs and started the day she hired them.

Henderson and Garrison had helped, going out to some of the bigger-name columnists and bringing them in.

Together with the other editors, she'd set up a stylebook and code of ethics. They hired some of the best fact checkers in the business, and nothing made it on the website until it had gone through three editors and at least one of the fact checkers. Every source was vetted.

Closing her laptop, she stuck it in the messenger bag. The lovely leather case had been waiting for her in her apartment when she'd first arrived. A gift from her marine. She'd received one at the apartment each day when she returned home. They had a routine that after dinner, they'd sit down and watch one of Harley's shows while they video chatted.

That hour each night had been her saving grace. It was almost like meditation, separating her from the stress at work and the time she needed to sleep. Not that she did much of that. After they signed off each night, she'd crash. Then she'd wake up at three in the morning to get to the office for the morning edition. There were a couple of nights when she was still at the office at nine. Still, she'd opened up the chat line and she and Blake had talked for more than an hour.

As she punched the button on the elevator, she realized she'd forgotten the flash drive of the confidential employee reports Henderson had given to her. She grabbed it quickly, she didn't want to keep her driver waiting downstairs as it was beginning to snow. Everyone had warned her that with the Thanksgiving holiday coming up in two weeks, and the weather, the weekend would likely turn a bustling Manhattan into a mess. The group's offices were located at Central Park West. She had a small space, but it had a prime view of the park. She didn't care about the size of her office. She'd expected to be in the middle of the newsroom.

But it was nice to have her privacy. By the time she returned to the elevator, it'd moved on. Being so high up it took a while—especially at the end of the day—to get an elevator.

Pushing the button again, she waited.

This time when the doors opened, Garrison stood there.

"Excellent. The boss wants to see us upstairs." He reached out and tugged her into the elevator. She landed against his chest.

"Hands off," she bit out.

"What? Does my intense charm send your senses reeling?" His mocking tone only annoyed her more.

"Uh, no. It definitely does *not*." She stepped to the other side of the elevator.

"You probably don't want to hear it from me, but you've done an amazing job this week." He sounded almost sincere.

"I appreciate your help with Appleton and Carter," she said, mentioning the two popular columnists he'd brought into the fold.

"Didn't have anything to do with me, it's this *mission*—there's no better word for it—that you're—we're—on."

She shrugged. "We're all fed up with the way things have been going with online journalism the past ten years. I only hope a lot of other online publications follow what we're doing."

The elevator doors slid open at the top floor. She and Garrison made their way to the double-etched glass doors that led to Henderson's sanctuary. That was what he called it. It was part office, part art gallery. The man had a passion for painting and sculpture. He'd insisted the arts get equal coverage as the headline grabbing news, which was fine by her.

"And here she is," Henderson said as they entered his inner office. He was there with some of the board members and a couple of vice presidents. He oversaw an entertainment conglomerate that had everything from television shows and films, to online video streaming sites, radio stations and a lot more.

He'd told her, that by hiring people like her, he was able to juggle so many things. "Hire the best," he said. "A hard worker is worth their weight." He had a soft spot for newspapers, which was why he was so interested in investing in the online industry.

Those assembled clapped as she joined them.

Okay, she should have dressed nicer. She'd run out of skirts and tops, and had worn her dark jeans with a T-shirt and jacket. The people around her were in suits, and the women wore dresses that weren't off the rack.

"You've made a tremendous difference and only a week's gone by," Henderson said as he handed her a glass of champagne. "If you folks will excuse us for a minute, I need to speak with our golden girl— pardon me—golden woman," he corrected when one of the women tsk-tsked.

"Sorry. You're a powerhouse. I didn't mean anything derogatory."

"No problem," she said as he ushered her into a conference room adjoining his office. It was almost as large as the reception area outside. The room had the same view as her office, although this was much more expansive.

"I have an instinct when it comes to people," he said as he motioned for her to have a seat at the table. "I was surprised when you left the Boston paper so fast. You were kind last week when I asked you about why. In the end, I found out the truth from one of the other interns who was working there at the time."

She started to speak, but he held up a hand.

"None of it matters now. But I've been doing a little more digging, and before I bring you into this next project, I have to ask you something personal again."

Great, now what? He was a handsome man, she only prayed he didn't hit on her.

He smiled as if he'd read her mind. "Don't worry. It's not like that. I just need to know if there's anything coming up in the next year that might pull your focus."

She frowned. "I'm not sure I understand."

"The marine? Great guy if the reports are to be believed. He's keeping an eye on the paper, oh, and your dog, while you're here, right?"

Chewing on her lip, she thought for a moment. "This is invasive, Aaron, Mr. Henderson. Would you ask a man the same thing?"

He chuckled. "Actually, I would. I have big plans for you, Macy. Your vision and leadership as well as your management skills are outstanding, and we'd like to take them—you—to the next level."

She blew out a breath.

"Over the next year, the plan is to transition you into a vice president's position overseeing your own division."

Wow.

"I'm not really the executive type." She glanced down at her jeans. "I—"

"*You* are perfect because you care about what's important, and we have a serious lack of people like you in the world. So then, you'll understand why I need to know if you're planning to get married and have children.

"And yes, I'd be asking the same if a man were sitting in your seat. This next year is key if we want to successfully implement a number of changes and do so as fast as possible. A vice presidency will mean a lot of travel for you and long days."

Marriage? Geez. She'd only known Blake for a month, though they both admitted they couldn't ever remember not loving each other.

"Some day, maybe," she said hesitantly. "But not anytime soon."

"Would it make it easier if we moved him here and offered him a position?"

That made her laugh. "Uh, no. That isn't a good idea. He has his hands full with a couple of businesses already, one of which he's responsible for getting off the ground. We're committed to one another, but that's all I can say for now. He's incredibly supportive of my choices. At some point, when I figure out the lay of the land here, I'll think about finding more permanent digs so at least Harley can join me."

"That's the Dane?"

She nodded.

He got out his wallet. "These are mine," he said, pointing at a photo of a pair of Irish wolfhounds.

"Amazing. They're bigger than Harley."

"Not by much, I'm sure. Those two keep me sane, and they go everywhere with me, even overseas."

She paused, about to speak.

"With enough money, you can make anything happen," he said, laughing as he pocketed his wallet.

"What I'm trying to say—although I'm not doing a very good job of it—is that we'll work with you when it comes to the personal business. If you need to fly your marine and Harley in for a visit, or have them travel with you anytime, that won't be a problem."

"But this kind of thing just doesn't happen to me. Ever," she said. What he was proposing seemed so surreal to her. "I'm the one who gets the rotten assignments, pinches her nose and moves on to the next story. I'm not used to being treated—"

"Special." He grinned.

"Yes. And besides, I don't understand it. We've recently hired a slew of talented journalists, why me? I asked you that question when you offered me the job, but I really need to know the answer."

He crossed his arms, and glanced out the window. "Because none of them have your passion for what we're doing. They want to be involved, but it takes someone like you to get others to take action. Not everyone has that. You do, and you have more potential than anyone I've ever hired. I wouldn't be surprised if you were doing my job some day."

That made her laugh. "As if." Then she covered her mouth with her hand. "Sorry."

He smiled warmly. "You have only one flaw. You're too hard on yourself. You've put in the hours, done a good job and now opportunity has come your way. How you handle your new responsibilities is up to you. Just remember, we're all human. And even the best of us make mistakes."

She wasn't sure why the conversation had taken this turn. "Did I do something wrong?"

He chuckled again. "No. But you have some tough decisions to make. I know it's a lot to take in your first week around here, but I wanted to make sure you were aware of what's ahead. That way you can plan your strategy. Will you be one of those people who have to decide how to wear many hats? Or will you be married to the job like me? And for the record, there's no wrong answer. I just want you to go forward fully informed of what's expected."

By the time she finished her glass of champagne and snuck out of the reception he'd thrown for her, it was nearly nine. She returned to her office, dealt with a few emails, collected her things and was completely and supremely grateful for the waiting chauffeur when she spotted him.

In the car, she called Blake, but he didn't answer. He was probably in the shower or out walking Harley. When she walked into her apartment, she smiled. There two dozen red roses with a card.

You made it to Friday. We knew you could do it.
Love B & H

She so appreciated Blake's thoughtfulness. After
a quick shower, she checked her phone. He hadn't
called or texted her back. After ringing the landline
at her house and getting no answer, she pulled back
her covers and snuggled into bed.

Too much information today. And more than anything she wanted to speak with Blake about it all, especially Henderson's plans for her. She texted Blake
one more time and then put her headphones on. Opening her laptop, she began editing a long column about
medical research funding.

By eleven, he still hadn't contacted her. It was only
ten in his time zone, but she worried that something
might be wrong. He was usually so good at returning her calls and texts.

She was about to call his mom, when her phone
rang.

"Hello, gorgeous woman of mine!"

"Hey, Marine. Thank you for the flowers."

She could hear a lot of people in the background.
Was he at a party?

"You deserve them. I called earlier but your assistant said they were throwing you a reception. I wanted
to let you know that I'm at a birthday party for my
brother. And don't worry about Harley. She's here
with me. She's the belle of the ball. Everyone keeps
telling her how beautiful she is. And of course, she
treats them like the adoring fans they are. We got a

great picture of her wearing a birthday hat. And Jaime made dog cupcakes for Harley and Bruno.

"Dog cupcakes. Can you believe it? What is the world coming to?"

That made her grin. "Why am I not surprised?"

"Sorry I didn't notice your first couple of texts. It's so loud. I couldn't hear my phone. I came outside with Harley, and noticed them. Is everything okay?"

He was out having a good time, and the last thing she wanted to do was ruin his fun with a heavy talk about their future.

"Yes, I just missed you. I want your arms around me."

"We are like-minded that way," he said.

"Blakeeeee, it's your turn," a woman's voice called out.

Blakeeee? Her stomach dropped.

"Well, I guess I better get going. I don't want to hold up the game. Can I call you in the morning? Or maybe we can V-chat?"

"Absolutely," she replied, forcing herself to sound positive. "Have fun tonight."

"I love you," he said, but he hung up before she could say it back.

It was silly for her to be upset. It was his brother's birthday party.

When had she become a woman who was jealous of someone having a little fun? If she'd really needed him, he would have dropped everything to talk to her. That knowledge should have been enough.

But how long could they do the long-distance relationship? So many times the past week, she'd wished

he were there for her to come home to. Selfish, perhaps, but she'd never really been in love. She thought
she was in love with Garrison, but now she knew it
wasn't anywhere close to the real thing.

*It's been only a week, and already you have
doubts? You're tired. Go to sleep.*

But her dreams were filled with Blake dancing
with a bevy of sexy, sultry women. She woke up
cranky and when Blake called, she didn't answer.
After going for a run and working out at the gym,
she realized how ridiculous she'd acted.

It had only been a week. She needed to get a grip.
Walking away from her marine was not an option,
but she also wouldn't give up the incredible chance
she'd been offered.

Picking up the phone, she called Blake.

"WELL, BABE, IT'S no wonder you feel overwhelmed,"
Blake said as he listened to Macy vent. Between her
job and everything else she had going on, she needed
him.

He'd hop on the first plane, but he had half a dozen
important business meetings set up over the next few
weeks.

"Thank you," she said. "I'm sorry it all kind of
poured out. I'm embarrassed about feeling so inse-
cure last night."

"Don't be. By the way that was Tanya from the
feed store giving me a hard time at the party. She
knew you were on the phone. There's only one woman
for me, and that's you. In fact, every time I walk down

the street, people ask how you're doing. You definitely left an impression."

She laughed. "I needed to hear that. And tell Tanya I'm going to get even with her when I see her."

"Noted," he said and laughed with her. He was glad to lighten up her mood.

"I am not this woman," she proclaimed and then sighed. "You know the one who gets jealous and is whiny. It's so selfish of me to want you here when you have a lot on your plate, and besides, I'm so busy that I fall into bed every night and get up before the sun. I think I might be addicted to you. I need those arms around me when I go to sleep."

"Hey, I feel the same. And if you were here, Harley would be less likely to crawl on your side of the bed in the middle of the night. I woke up this morning and couldn't breathe. Her head was on my stomach. Oh, and this is where I found her yesterday afternoon."

She put him on speaker and opened the text when it arrived. The bed was made, but Harley's head was on her pillow.

"I think she might miss you a little." Blake chuckled. "Every once in a while, I find her in your closet. She's just lying in there on a pile of your clothes. I kept washing stuff, but finally gave up. I found some of your old pj's and sweatshirts and made a small pile in the middle of the closet for her."

"That's sweet. I miss you both so much it makes my heart hurt."

"I'm right there with you. Give yourself some grace. Any job is tough that first month, but it's obvious given what he's offering you after one week, that they really believe in you. I know I do. Is this a crazy route to starting a relationship? Yes. But we aren't like everyone else. And honestly, if I stayed in the marines, we would have had to have been separated even longer."

"True. I feel better just talking to you."

"Next time you feel like you did last night, don't be afraid to tell me that you need me. You're there for me and I'm here for you. Don't forget that. Also, any hope of you getting away for Thanksgiving?"

"I hadn't even thought about the holidays much. They're coming up fast—maybe I'll be home for Christmas. But there's still a lot to do here the next couple of weeks. And I've never been a huge fan of Thanksgiving. My parents didn't really do holidays."

Another hiccup. He'd promised his mother he'd be home for this Thanksgiving. It would be the first one in eight years he'd make. He wouldn't disappoint his mom. But even though she put up a good front, Macy needed him more.

"No problem. Christmas will be great," he said without enthusiasm.

It wasn't his favorite option, but that was the way things were.

"It isn't lost on me how lucky I am to have you in my life," she said softly.

"I know and I feel the same, Macy." But he was worried that the longer they were apart, the more she'd withdraw. She was so used to being on her own that she didn't feel comfortable coming to him when she was stressed or having a bad day. Clearly, she thought she should only show him the good side.

No way would he let her do that. It would mean sacrifice on his part, but Macy was worth it. He thought they could wait it out longer. But she needed him now, if for no other reason than to have someone be there for her at the end of the day. And he was the only someone who would be doing that.

After they hung up, he called his brother.

"We need to talk."

18

"Do you need me to stay?" Joe Pollack, Macy's assistant, glanced at the heavy snow falling outside her office window. She knew he had plans to catch a train and travel upstate to see his family for the holiday.

"No, you go ahead. I'll do a final check on the new sites to make sure there are no bugs, and then I'll be leaving, too."

"Thanks. You do know that Stu and Margaret have been through those sites multiple times today? They're clean, and they even added several upgraded firewalls to make it tougher for the hackers."

Shuffling papers on her desk, she looked up at him. "You know how I am. Once I feel like everyone really understands how important speed *and* accuracy and all of this is, I promise, I'll cut back on the micromanaging."

Joe didn't seem convinced. "Right. That's never going to happen."

She smiled. She couldn't help it. "I've been a bit on the loony side, have I?"

"I wouldn't say loony, more like determined. Uh, very determined."

"Always a diplomat. That's why you are such a super assistant."

"Yes, that and my ability to know when you are in need of coffee. Oh, and let's not forget my special talent to keep you from chewing out those who displease you," he joked, taking the bite out of his words. She'd had run-ins with a few reporters who hadn't double-checked their facts. The stories had been minutes away from going up on the site, when one of the fact checkers had called her to relay the news that there was something wrong.

Macy understood and appreciated the fact checker speaking up, but she made it clear, anyway, that those kinds of mistakes wouldn't be tolerated. Joe had remained at her side just to make sure she didn't actually throttle the reporters.

Admittedly it had been a good idea. One incorrect story could ruin everything they were all working so hard to achieve.

"Don't stay too late. Are you sure you don't want to come with me? My mom's always insisting there's room for one more at the table. She'd love to meet you."

"That's so nice of you, Joe. And I'd love to meet your mom. Be sure to arrange it if she's ever here visiting you. Thanks, anyway, but I'm looking forward to sleeping for a good twenty-four hours. I can't remember the last time I slept in."

He nodded. "You're always the last to leave and

first to arrive. There's been gossip that you actually live here."

"Sometimes it feels like it."

"Did you know, that if you were so inclined, your office has a perfect view of the Thanksgiving Parade?"

No, she didn't know that. Maybe she would come into the office, after all. Other than sleeping, she really didn't have anything else to do. "Cool. Now go on. The crowds at the station are going to be horrible. I don't want you to miss your train."

After he left, she sat back in her chair and blew out a breath. Everyone had worked so hard earlier in the week so they could be with their families. Even Henderson had taken off for Barbados to get away from the subzero temperature.

Even Cherie had abandoned her. She was on a book tour in Europe. Macy had seen her friend only once since arriving in New York. Cherie's book about relationships had hit the bestseller lists and she was more popular than ever.

Macy's cell rang. She glanced at the picture that came up on the mini screen and smiled.

"Hello, Mr. Marine."

"Hello, yourself. Are you still at work?"

"I am, though I did promise myself I'd leave before it gets too late. The weather is taking a turn for the worse."

He coughed. "I heard. I was worried about you getting home."

"Ah, you're too kind. Tony will be here to pick

me up. You don't need to worry. How is everything going with you? Is your mom fixing a huge feast?"

He snorted. "You said, 'fixing.' Our Texas words have seeped into your vocabulary, as for Mom, enough food for five or six families. We were over there the other day and discovered that Harley has a thing for apple pies."

"Oh, no. She didn't."

"She did. But we caught her before she ate the second one off the counter. She didn't feel so good for a day or two, but the vet says she's fine. I was going to tell you about it, but you had so much going on that I didn't want to possibly add to your concerns."

"You have a ton of patience. I don't know how you put up with her like you do."

"I don't consider her a chore. She's fun to have around."

She could hear Harley barking in the background as if confirming the fact.

Macy froze. She wanted to be there with them. Her mouth watered at the idea of homemade apple pie. It was stupid of her to stay in New York. Most of what she had to do was online. She could have gone home.

But it was too late now.

It was the day before Thanksgiving, no way would she be able to find a flight. And the company jet was in Barbados with Henderson. Even if a flight was available, with the snow the way it was, she had little chance of getting out of the city.

"Hey, did I lose you?"

"No. Sorry. I was just thinking how silly I am for

not coming home to see you at Thanksgiving. Work is busy, but—"

"Don't beat yourself up," he said. "If I hadn't promised my mom that I'd spend the holiday with her, I'd be dragging you out of that office right now."

Harley barked again.

"What's going on?"

"She needs to go out. Can I call you back? Or call me when you're on your way home so I know you're safe." He sounded distracted. Well, he probably was. Harley was likely dragging him to the door.

"No problem. I'll call from the apartment once I get there. Love you."

"Love you, too."

Chewing on her lip, she decided to pack it in. Poor Tony probably had a family he'd like to get home to, as well. She could work from her place. If she wanted to. After texting Tony, to let him know that she was ready to leave, she headed out.

In the lobby, she ran into Garrison, who held two bags of food. "Macy, I was just bringing these things up to you. I found this Thai restaurant still open nearby. Your assistant told me you'd be working tonight."

Her ex had been a little too nice the past few weeks, which made her suspicious. But he'd kept it professional, and Henderson had mentioned that his reports about her had been complimentary.

"Can I ask you something?"

He looked surprised. "Sure."

"What's up? Why are you being so considerate, when you've always been so competitive? I half expected you to tell Aaron that I was doing an awful job."

He shrugged. "I may be a cheating jerk, but even I can't deny you're as talented as they come. Besides, he doesn't need any reports from me. The evidence is out there. It's admirable what you've done. And honestly, I've been nice, because I have this horrible fear that you might be my boss some day. He's that impressed with you."

She laughed. "Oh, geez. You're serious aren't you?"

He nodded.

"Well, you don't need to worry. I forgive your past transgressions. I'm in a really good place. I'm happy in my relationship right now. It isn't easy, us being apart so much, but we're making it work."

He smiled. "I'm truly happy for you. Really. You deserve happiness. He's a fortunate guy."

"Thanks. Sorry about dinner, but I'm on my way home." She stared at the bags. "I have plans."

This was Garrison's life. Take-out Thai food the night before Thanksgiving while he worked. All of a sudden she knew that wasn't the life she wanted for herself. It was so clear to her now.

Henderson had asked if she'd be the kind of person who would learn to wear many hats. She was. Because she didn't want to end up lonely like the man in front of her, or like Henderson, for that matter.

"With who?"

"Huh?"

"Who are your plans with?"

The thought struck her as funny because it was so

glaringly obvious, and she laughed. "Don't look so surprised. My boyfriend."

"I thought he was in Texas." He seemed confused.

"Have a good Thanksgiving, Garrison. See you Monday."

With that she was out the door. Maybe she couldn't be in Texas, but they could share a virtual Thanksgiving. It was better than nothing. She couldn't wait to get back to the apartment and tell Blake her idea.

The snow was pretty, though it fell fast and didn't look to be letting up anytime soon. It took an extra half hour to reach her building.

"Tony, stay in the car. You don't need to open the door. And thank you. Have a wonderful holiday."

He turned to face her. "Won't you be needing me?"

She shook her head. "Not this weekend. You take some well-deserved time off. Enjoy."

He tipped his hat to her, and the doorman opened the car door. "Mind your step, miss. It's very slick on the sidewalk." He carefully led her to the front door. The soles of her boots were smooth, and made the slippery walk treacherous even with his help.

"Thanks," she said as she entered into the lobby. The marble floors proved to be as slick as the sidewalk. Just inside the door she slipped, and would have fallen if strong arms hadn't held her up.

"Whoa," a deep voice said.

It couldn't be.

Her marine smiled down at her. Had she fallen and woken in a dream? This could not be real.

"You— It's not—"

He kissed her then, and she lost herself in his embrace.

Harley barked and barked beside them.

"Ah, sweet girl." Macy bent down to put her arms around the dog's massive neck. "I've missed you."

She stood and stared at Blake, her heart soaring. Blake touched her cheek. "How is it you haven't been sleeping, yet you're still so damn beautiful?"

"Also sweet. But how did you get here? Not that I'm complaining." Macy wished the doorman a happy Thanksgiving and she, Blake and Harley headed for the elevator.

"Well, you couldn't come to Thanksgiving, so I brought Thanksgiving to you." He gave her that sexy smile of his and inside she melted a little. She loved this man.

"I can't believe you're here. I feel like time has stood still or something and suddenly I'm going to find out that none of this is really happening. And I do so want it to be happening."

He chuckled. "Let's get upstairs and I'll show you just how real it is," he whispered.

She sighed happily. "How was she on the plane?" With the loud noises, Macy was surprised the dog still wasn't sleepy.

"We drove," he said. "I didn't have the heart to put her in the cargo hold. And I had some business in North Carolina. We've been on the road the last few days."

"Why didn't you tell me!" she said as she pushed the button for her floor. "I was searching for flights while we were on the phone, but it was ridiculous considering this is the busiest day of the year."

"That and the airports are shut down." He gathered her in his arms. "We wanted to surprise you."

"You did." Her heart felt light. She was excited and at peace all at once. "Surreal. This is what it feels like. There's no better word for it. Wait, Harley's on the elevator, but pets aren't allowed in the building."

"She is. Evidently, she's the exception."

"I bet Henderson had something to do with that. He's a big fan of dogs."

"She did get me into your apartment. I hope that's okay. I had some things to drop off there before I could find a place to park and walk the dog."

"Make yourself at home. Whatever I have is yours."

She opened the door and was assailed by the smell of delicious food.

She turned to glance at him, and he shrugged. In her kitchen, she found his mother and brother, up to their elbows in dressing.

Throwing her arms about their necks, she kissed each of them on the cheek. "I'm so happy you're here. I can't believe you guys did this. Thank you, thank you."

"It's nothing, dear," his mother said, smiling. "Let me get my hands out of this corn bread, and I'll give you a proper hug."

She looked up at Blake who smiled at her.

"You did all of this. How?"

"Harley and I drove, but Mom and J.T. flew in this morning. We knew about the weather. They've been cooking all day. You're a part of the family now, and it wouldn't be right to celebrate without you. Besides, we heard you have an excellent spot to watch the Thanksgiving Parade. Mom's a fan, so she had no problem packing everything in dry ice and shipping it here."

Macy put her hands to her cheeks. "No one's ever done anything like this for me. You guys are incredible."

"It's what families do," J.T. said as he nudged her with his shoulder.

"Why don't you and Blake relax? Dinner should arrive in just a bit," his mother said.

Macy was baffled.

"All of this," J.T. said, waving at the cluttered counter, "is for tomorrow's lunch. We ordered pizza for tonight. It's a family tradition, or at least it was when Blake and I were kids. Mom was always too busy getting ready for the big day to take time to cook dinner the night before, so our dad would order pizza. And there's no better place to carry on that tradition than here."

Thankfully, the kitchen was well stocked with dishes and pots and pans, none of which had been used since she'd moved in. Most of her meals were eaten at work, and then she'd order in most nights.

But sitting around the dining room table with Blake's family, well, it was the best gift anyone could have given her. The brothers gave each other a hard time, their mom butting in to tell them to behave. They were a proper family.

Her parents loved her and cared about her, but they

didn't understand the importance of having this kind of time together.

She wouldn't make that mistake. Macy wanted it all. The family squabbles, the general silliness that came with hanging out with people who knew you better than you knew yourself—and the love.

A few hours later, she and Blake were in bed. Harley had passed out in the living room, and Blake's mom and brother had gone to their hotel.

"I know I keep saying this, but I still can't believe you are here."

He put an arm around her shoulders and leaned over for a kiss. "Believe it," he said and he kissed her again. Desire pooled in her belly. Yes, this was the way one should end the day.

His hand curved around her hip, and he drew her nearer. Wrapping his arms around her, he held her tight.

"This is home," she said against his chest.

He kissed her mouth, her cheek, behind her ear. "Yes, that's the way I feel. It doesn't matter where we live, as long as we're together." He went back to kissing her lips.

"I've got to tell you something, Blake, so just listen, okay? You don't have to say anything."

Blake tensed.

"I mean it. Just listen to what I have to say." She poked his chest as she glanced up at him. "I need to do this before I chicken out."

"Okaaaay," he said slowly.

She met his eyes. "I love you, Blake Michaels. And I want it all."

As her words sunk in, a slow smile split across his face.

"That's a good thing, since I love you and I want it all. In fact, I'm willing to do whatever it takes to make that happen."

"Wait." She lifted her head. "What are *you* saying?"

He gave her a sheepish grin. "I've been making a lot of changes over the last few weeks. I wanted to tell you, but it wasn't until a few days ago that I knew everything was going to fall into place the way I wanted it to. As long as you're all right with what I'm about to ask."

What was he talking about? What kind of changes? "You can ask me anything," she said honestly.

"How would you feel about Harley and I moving here full-time?"

Uh, it would be a dream come true. She slugged his arm. "How do you think I'd feel?"

"Hey, no need for violence." He rolled over and pulled her on top of him.

"I can't believe you were making all these plans and didn't tell me. I've been devising all these scenarios trying to figure out how I can split my time between here and Texas." She sat up straighter, fully aware that he was hard as a rock underneath her.

"So you like the idea."

She laughed. "Of course. It's what I've wanted all along, but I didn't feel right asking you to give up everything you had there to move here with me."

"If you'd asked, I would have done it. But a couple of weeks ago when you were so sad, I realized I didn't care if you wanted me to be here or not, you needed me. I'd do anything for you." He took her wrist and brought her forward and kissed her.

"I want and need you," she whispered, "more than you will ever know."

"Trust me, I do know. I'll have to go back and forth for a while. J.T. will help me out. I'll be based here, though. And it's good timing, too, for the security business my friends and I have. We're thinking of expanding and opening an office here. Besides my financial duties, the guys want me to take charge of implementing the new ideas we've got going and do a forecast for a possible office here. It's a lot, but as soon as I made the decision to be here with you, it all fell into place."

She kissed him, lightly at first, and then she deepened the kiss, putting everything she had into it. "I'm so glad. And what about you know who?" she asked.

He twisted one of her curls around his finger. "You know who will be happy having us and her toys. At some point we should maybe consider trying to find a house outside the city, but there's a great dog park not far from here. She loved it."

"You really have thought of everything."

Something was still making her nervous, and she realized it was because she was so happy.

"You don't think it's too soon for us to cohabitate?" he asked, his expression serious.

She shook her head. "You know it isn't. Like you said, there may be some bumps along the way, but if you're riding over them with me, we can cruise through life together."

"That was a terrible metaphor." He laughed.

"Yes. Yes, it was."

"Have I mentioned how much I love you?"

She glanced at the nonexistent watch on her wrist. "It has been a good ten minutes since the last time. I was beginning to wonder."

Growling, he reversed their positions.

She smiled, and put her hands on either side of his face to hold him close. "Show me, Blake," she said, "show me how much you love me."

Capturing her lips in a long and passionate kiss, he left her breathless. Just from the kiss alone she was ready for him.

"Not so fast, sweetheart," he said as he nuzzled her neck. His mouth paid equal attention to each of her breasts. As he moved down, kissing all the way, she cried out. Having him here with her meant everything to her.

He caressed her, tempted her, touched her exactly as she wanted to be touched. He was amazing, so strong and also so tender.

Her orgasm was searing and swift. She felt it from her head to the tips of her toes. It made her shudder and call out his name.

"Now," she said, shutting her eyes, anticipating him.

"No." He teased her into yet another orgasm. This one robbed her of all control. "Blake, Blake…" she whispered.

He stroked her thighs, moving onto his knees. The intensity of passion in his gaze was enough to make her shudder again.

He entered her slowly, carefully, filling her, completing her.

"Yes," she said, matching the intimate movement of his hips.

As they raced to the edge together and leaped, he kissed her thoroughly. Every bit of love he felt for her was in that kiss, and she returned it.

He was her marine, body and soul.

19

HARLEY BARKED AS Santa passed by the window. Blake's mom clapped, and the woman wrapped in his arms laughed so hard he couldn't help but smile. They were all in Macy's office enjoying the parade.

J.T. shook his head in wonder. "How does she know it's Santa?" he asked.

"Who knows? But she does have a thing for presents and toys," Macy answered.

They laughed.

"Dear girl, that parade was too exquisite for words," Blake's mom said. "So much better in person and beyond anything I could imagine. I am surprised that even with all the snow on the sidewalks, so many people showed up."

"Yes. It was fun and nice to be able to watch it here in my office where it's warm and comfortable. More snow is expected later this afternoon. I'm just glad the skies cleared a bit so they could have the parade. It would have been awful if you came all this way to see it, and then it didn't happen."

His mother pulled her out of Blake's arms and

hugged her. "Macy, sweetie, we didn't come for the parade. We came to see you. No one should be alone on Thanksgiving. I've had a few too many of those myself, and I didn't want that for you." She kissed Macy's cheek. "Let's roll, J.T., we'll take Harley for a walk. You two be back at Macy's place by one so we can eat."

She paused in front of Blake and touched his hand. "It's wonderful to see you so happy, son. It's about time."

He held his mom's hand and squeezed. "Mom, you are the absolute best. I love you."

"Love you, too, son. Don't be late for dinner." She followed J.T. and Harley out the door.

Blake sat on the edge of Macy's desk. She pushed his legs apart and slipped in between them. He leaned toward her and she put her arms around his neck and kissed him.

"This has been on of the best days of my life and it's still early."

He held her close. "I agree. Are you sure you're okay with my family invading your space unannounced?" He'd kept an eye on her throughout the morning. It was almost as if she were afraid of offending someone or saying the wrong thing. He didn't want her to feel that way.

"Blake, I so appreciate what your mom and brother have done for me this Thanksgiving. It's been great. I've never felt like—I was a part of a family. Years on my own, well, you know how it's been. Now that I see what I've been missing out on, I want to make up for lost time. So there's no invasion. I'm ecstatic that you and your family are here."

He kissed her nose. "Good. Because my mom is

very excited about shopping tomorrow. I was hoping I could count on you to handle that one."

Macy laughed. "Always with the ulterior motives. I should have known. But if I'm going out in the wilds of Manhattan and facing all those shoppers, then seriously, you're coming with us." She tugged on his arm and they left her office.

"I had a feeling you'd say that." At the elevator, he helped her on with her coat. He thought about that and all the other things in future that he would want to help her with. Big and small. He planned to spend the rest of his life loving this woman.

She was his everything.

One day he'd ask her to marry him, but not until he knew she was ready. The year ahead represented a lot of change for her. He'd be there for her. He wanted her to achieve her dreams. In fact, he couldn't think of anywhere he'd rather be.

"Hey, Mr. Deep Thoughts. What's going on in that brain of yours?" She was standing in the elevator, waiting for him.

No more living day to day, wondering if it might be his last. From now on he and Macy lived in a world of possibility.

"I'm thinking about the interesting things I can do with you after everyone leaves tonight."

Her cheeks turned a bright shade of pink as she yanked him into the elevator. "Now that's all I'm going to think about during dinner."

He waggled his eyebrows. And then he kissed her.

This was only the start of a long and happy life together.

* * * * *

COMING NEXT MONTH FROM

Available November 19, 2013

#775 COWBOYS & ANGELS
Sons of Chance
by Vicki Lewis Thompson
The last person ranch hand Trey Wheeler expects to meet at a ski lodge is the woman who saved him from a car crash. Elle Masterson is way more tempting than your average guardian angel—and Trey wants to be tempted....

#776 A SOLDIER'S CHRISTMAS
Uniformly Hot!
by Leslie Kelly, Joanne Rock and Karen Foley
When they come home for Christmas, three military heroes have visions in their heads of things far sexier than sugarplums. But the women they love want more than just one very good night....

#777 THE MIGHTY QUINNS: DEX
The Mighty Quinns
by Kate Hoffmann
When Irish news cameraman Dex Kennedy takes on a documentary project, he doesn't realize that the job will uncover some startling family secrets—and put him in the path of a sexy American producer who is all business. Except in the bedroom!

#778 NAUGHTY CHRISTMAS NIGHTS
by Tawny Weber
Romance vs sex? Designer Hailey North is determined her lacy lingerie will be the new holiday line at Rudolph's Department Stores. Gage Milano is providing competition with his hot leather look. But in the nights leading up to Christmas, things are heating up—between Hailey and Gage!

YOU CAN FIND MORE INFORMATION ON UPCOMING HARLEQUIN® TITLES, FREE EXCERPTS AND MORE AT WWW.HARLEQUIN.COM.

HBCNM1113

REQUEST YOUR FREE BOOKS!
2 FREE NOVELS PLUS 2 FREE GIFTS!

red-hot reads!

"We can't kiss again. We have to keep things strictly professional from here on out."

"Of course," Dex said. "I completely agree. And I can do that." He grabbed Marlie's hand and pulled her back down next to him.

They stared at each other for a long moment. "You're thinking about kissing me again, aren't you?" She sighed softly. "Maybe we just ought to do it again so we can move on."

Dex nodded. "You're right, it probably would help."

She drew a deep breath and forced a smile. "So, I guess you should just do it and get it over with."

"Right," Dex murmured.

Hell, he knew if he kissed her again, the attraction would never go away. It would just get worse. And then having to pretend that it didn't exist while they worked together would be pure torture. But he wasn't about to refuse her invitation. He wasn't a bloody eedjit.

Dex slipped his hand around her nape, his fingers tangling in her hair. He gently drew her close and touched his lips to hers. But the moment they made contact, he knew he was lost. A need so fierce, so overwhelming, surged up inside of him. He wanted to touch her, to kiss her, to tear her clothes off and make love to her until his body was exhausted and his mind was quiet.

Dex took a chance and pulled her even closer, his tongue teasing at her lips, searching for the warmth of her mouth and her unspoken surrender. When she opened beneath the assault, he groaned softly and drew her body on top of his, lying back on the sofa.

He needed this, a chance to clear his head of all the dark memories, all the twisted guilt that plagued his every waking minute. If he could just find some peace, if only for one night, maybe he could put his life back on track.

As their kiss grew more intense, Dex pulled her beneath him, desperate to feel her body against his. He stared down at her, his fingers brushing strands of hair from her face. Her lashes fluttered and the color was high in her cheeks. God, she was so beautiful, so perfect. The prospect of losing himself in her warmth was too tempting to deny.

She opened her eyes, their gazes meeting, and for a moment, he thought she was going to speak.

"What?" he murmured.

"I—I think that's enough," Marlie murmured.

"No," he whispered. "It's not nearly enough."

Pick up THE MIGHTY QUINNS: DEX by Kate Hoffmann, available November 19, wherever you buy Harlequin® Blaze® books.

HBEXP79781R